# A view from Niagara

**THE PROSE AND POEMS OF
JOAN WINIFRED BALLS** MBE
*With photographs by the Author*

©2004 Barbara Smith
*A View from Niagara*
ISBN 0-9548539-0-3

Published by:
Amen House Publications
7 Beryl Road
Bedminster
Bristol
BS3 3DH

The right of the executors of the author (Amen House Publications) to be identified as the owner of this work has been asserted by them in accordance with the Copyright, Designs and Patents Act 1988.

All rights reserved. No part of this publication may be produced in any form or by any means – graphic, electronic or mechanical including photocopying, recording, taping or information storage and retrieval systems – without prior permission in writing from the publisher.

A CIP catalogue for this book is available from the British Library.

Design and production co-ordinated by
The ***Better Book*** Company Ltd
Havant
Hampshire
PO9 2XH

Printed in England

Cover picture - a view from the harbour at Wells-next-the-Sea

# CONTENTS

| | |
|---|---|
| Foreword | Page 1 |
| Dedicatory Poem – 'Joan' | 3 |
| Acknowledgments | 4 |

## The Prose

| | |
|---|---|
| Once Upon a Time | Page 5 |
| A Happy Thing | 12 |
| Ghosts Don't Smell | 17 |
| Waterspell | 23 |
| The Outing | 26 |
| Watchdog | 30 |
| Lust | 35 |
| The Last Leaf | 36 |
| Cast a Long Shadow | 40 |
| The Apple Loft | 49 |
| The Corner Table | 53 |
| The Dog and Duck | 61 |
| Ceremony | 67 |

## The Poems

| | | | |
|---|---|---|---|
| Chrysalis | Page 83 | Puffball | Page 97 |
| Haiku 1 | 83 | Pebble | 97 |
| Night Lights | 84 | Barney's Shop | 98 |
| Age Speaks To Death | 84 | Poor Minnie Mouse | 100 |
| Dance With Me | 85 | Haiku 3 | 100 |
| The Loneliness Of Today | 86 | One Friday Afternoon | 101 |
| I Remember The Flowers | 86 | Kathy | 104 |
| Freedom | 87 | Fragment | 104 |
| Shy | 88 | The Meadow Fairy | 104 |
| Haiku 2 | 88 | Paradise, Once | 105 |
| The Trees Are Bare | 89 | The Only Permanence | 106 |
| November | 90 | Haiku 4/5 | 107 |
| The Golden Tree | 91 | They Do Not Come Here | 108 |
| A Brief Hiatus | 91 | Haiku 6 | 108 |
| A Non-Valentine | 93 | The Worst Winter | 109 |
| Inconsistency | 93 | The Mountain | 110 |
| Limericks | 94 | Haiku 7 | 111 |
| Cuthbert | 95 | Usually People Tether Goats | 112 |
| Suspension | 95 | Metamorphosis | 113 |
| Lovely Is My Love | 96 | The Call Of The Sea | 114 |
| Valentine | 96 | Farewell My Love | 115 |

*17 Niagara Avenue in 1934 – the author's home*

# Foreword

My family and I lived next door to Joan, her sister Evelyn and their father for four years. Sadly we never knew Florence, the wife and mother who died in 1957. They had lived at seventeen Niagara Avenue, Ealing, since the houses were built in 1934; March 28th to be precise. We had the happiest of relations with our neighbours and they became very good friends.

Even though my work changed, and after those four years we moved to Bristol, our friendship lasted over thirty years. We kept in regular contact and on occasion Joan drove to Bristol in her elegant and nearly classic car to visit us.

In 1970 we were delighted to read that Joan had been awarded the MBE in recognition of her work as an administrator in the Colonial Office – it is unlikely we would have heard of the award from Joan herself. Her father, Herbert, died in 1975 and her sister four years later.

After my wife Elsie died in 1990, I made several visits to Niagara Avenue, hearing with interest about the various hobbies Joan had taken up. Photography had always been high on her list of interests and she often sent me pictures of Norfolk – her favourite county. Lapidary, the art of polishing stones and mounting them in jewellery, was a later pastime she greatly enjoyed. However, there is no doubt in my mind that the greatest pleasure she derived was from the writing group she joined. Joan produced many fine pieces of poetry and prose and had several poems published in *Poetry Ealing*, the local magazine. Although she suffered failing eyesight, this never sapped her enthusiasm for doing what she enjoyed.

In 1996 Joan attended our wedding service, when Elizabeth and I were married, and another strong friendship was formed. Early in September last year (2003) we were told that Joan had sustained an injury from an accident, following which she underwent an operation. Sadly she suffered a heart attack and, although she survived a month, unhappily she never recovered consciousness and died on October 1st.

The funeral on October 8th was attended by her close friends, including the writers who read poems either by or about Joan. Her godson, John Henn, spoke of her constant generosity. We were also reminded of her love of cats: 'She was mighty fond of cats,' said the Reverend Cecil Smith, in his moving tribute that reflected Joan's full and rewarding life.

On the grey and chilly morning of 29th November a few of us gathered on the quayside at Wells-next-the-Sea in Norfolk, a place Joan had loved. One friend said it was her spiritual home. We had gathered there to carry out her final wish. The Harbour Master took us out in his launch for a short way and, after reading Joan's poem, *Farewell my Love*, I cast her ashes upon the waters.

May this volume be a fitting memorial to

## Joan Winifred Balls MBE

A gifted, generous and kind lady whom it was a pleasure to have known and to have been numbered among her friends

*Rex Hipple - December 2004*

# *Joan*

She was lying under a wardrobe. A small wardrobe,
Light and easy to move, easy to pull down.
Even if you were old and small
And lost your balance trying to open it.
Hard to lift off if you were old and fat and had nowhere to stand.
We waited for the ambulance: ten minutes for my watch,
An hour for me and an age for her.

She was lying in the ward.
'Perfectly comfortable!' she lied, as she dictated a list:
Papers and milk to stop, people to tell,
Perishable foods to be thrown, stuff like that.
I made to leave but she stopped me: 'I hope you don't mind,
I've named you as my next-of-kin;
You see I've no family.' Apologising.

She was lying between the machines in the ICU.
I wore a disposable apron, torn like a Tesco's bag from a slab.
I'd declined the tea and chair, which would have prolonged the visit.
To avoid wasting the disposable rubber gloves,
I ventured a hand between the tubes. You're supposed to talk,
Poetry or politics or anything, but I couldn't chat
To a machine with such a small human component.

She was lying in Intensive Care. The stressed staff complained
Of the number of phone calls. 'Tell me about it!' I said,
Having spent hours talking to people from a dozen locations.
All were very concerned and some were distressed;
Only the twenty-year-old student from Luton cried
But others came close. I, her next-of-kin,
Was not surprised, for she had quite an extensive family.

*Richard Miller*

# *Acknowledgments*

The following of Joan Balls' poems were originally published in *Poetry Ealing*, the magazine of Pitshanger Poets: *Usually People Tether Goats, Suspension, Puffball, Valentine, Inconstancy, The Trees are Bare, Shy, Chrysalis* and *Age Speaks to Death*. Their appearance in this form is gratefully acknowledged.

Richard Miller's poem, *Joan*, was also published in *Poetry Ealing*.

The work of Eleanor Kamester, Richard Miller, Norman Silvester and Barbara Smith in researching, compiling and transcribing Joan's manuscripts was invaluable in making this volume possible.

*Rex Hipple*

The publishers gratefully acknowledge the generous support given by the charities benefiting from Joan's estate in the publication of this volume.

# *The Prose*

## *Once Upon a Time*

The highlight of my year when I was a child was our summer holiday. We always left the house by the back door. Father, who was a policeman, was very security-conscious and, by leaving the back way, he could shoot the inside bolt on the front door. On reflection I cannot see the logic of this, since the back of the house was far more vulnerable to break-in: we were not overlooked, except by a railway siding, and the back door, far less robust than the front, was the one where the inside bolts would have given greater protection. But perhaps he thought to make our departure less conspicuous than if we had trooped down the road, all four of us, with our baggage. So we went down the wide alley that ran behind our row of little terraced houses to a flight of stone steps that led up to the main road and the local railway station.

Our clothes and other requirements for the fortnight were packed into two suitcases, both of which Father carried. He would not accept help, saying that one in each hand gave an even balance. He was a big man, so probably the weight did not bother him: to me they were immovable. He was an excellent packer, every shoe was stuffed with something – socks, stockings, shaving brush, toothpaste, cream pots, and sundry other small items: not an inch of space was wasted. I watched and stored that expertise in my memory.

I do not remember much about the journey to Liverpool Street, but I remember the bustle and excitement of that main-line station: the smell peculiar to steam trains and the sight and sound of the hissing steam. It was a long journey to Norwich in those days – or it seemed so to me – but I was never bored: all the time we were drawing nearer and nearer to those halcyon days of sun, sand, sea and freedom ahead. I would sing "Strawberry Fair" to myself, over and over (once I was old enough to have learned it at school). The sheer gaiety of the tune so exactly suited the occasion.

We broke the journey at Norwich to spend a few hours with Father's parents. They lived in a tiny four-roomed cottage in Sprowston Road, near Mousehold Heath. The cottage had a minute front garden and the back yard – which I think was mainly paved – was not much bigger. A tram depot lay behind the cottage and the clanging of the trams made a constant background noise. For some reason I felt uneasy in that back yard and avoided it. Like Father, Grandfather was a big man, and rather intimidating with his white whiskers and beard. I am sure he was very kindly, but he was quite a lot older than Grandmother and died before I could know him properly. He had a wooden rocking chair with a seat highly polished by generations of trousers, and he liked to put me there and rock me. That seat seemed huge to me when I was very small; I covered no more than a quarter of it and, though I clung to the arms, I slithered uncomfortably backwards and forwards and was terrified of shooting off.

From Norwich we must have taken a local train to Stalham (on the Broads) but I don't remember it. From Stalham we covered the last few miles to Sea Palling by pony-trap. Once, later, when a few people had motor cars, we did the whole journey from Norwich by car with a man who lived in Palling but worked in Norwich. He had an open tourer and it was a hair-raising experience – literally. This man recognised only one method of driving, at full throttle and down the middle of the road. The wind tore at our faces and we clung to our hats with both hands. (Those were the days when one was not properly dressed without a hat, even on the beach). We rounded the sharp bend at Ingham on two wheels: the car bounced as it regained its equilibrium. I don't think we repeated the experience. Later still a bus ran between Norwich and Yarmouth, and Palling was on its route. The journey was liable to unscheduled stops and divergences if Mrs Smith wanted to drop a parcel in to her sister, or Mr Popay had asked the driver to call on his old mother to check that she was all right.

Sea Palling was (and still is) a very small village. We stayed in one of a row of four flint-walled cottages, which stood back to front; that is, the kitchens faced the road across a communal gravelled yard. The doors were always open. Behind the kitchen was the parlour with a dining table and over-stuffed uncomfortable chairs. This was the front of the cottage and looked on to a long garden full of fruit trees and currant bushes. From the corner of the parlour, seemingly in the thickness of the wall, a narrow staircase led to the two bedrooms above, which opened off one another: they smelled sweetly of lavender. At the bottom of all the gardens was a small wooden shed which housed the primitive toilet, for there was no sanitation, no piped water, no gas, and electricity had hardly been heard of. Water was pumped from a well a little way down the road. I loved to work the clanking pump handle, though my puny strength produced only a trickle of water. The shed in the garden was a frightening place, especially at night when you only had a candle to see by. The flickering light sent shadows dancing about the whitewashed walls and the constant movement suggested the scuttling of spiders. There were real spiders, too, in plenty and I was terrified of them. Torn-up newspaper served as toilet paper and, chemical disposal being unknown, someone had the unsavoury task of emptying the bucket each day. What happened to the contents I never cared to enquire.

The cottage was lit by oil lamps downstairs and by candles upstairs. A big old black cooking range took up the whole of one side of the tiny kitchen. It was an open fire behind bars with an oven built into the wall at its side and, although one would have thought the heat couldn't be controlled, it produced perfectly cooked meals. A smoke-encrusted kettle lived permanently on the hob.

These holidays were a gathering of family (Father's) and family friends. Auntie Edie and her husband Jim lived at Palling, in the cottage next door to the one where we stayed. Auntie Kate and Uncle George from Norwich stayed with her. Their friends, the Easters, and

Uncle Ernie and his family from London stayed nearby. Auntie Kate and Uncle George, Uncle Ernie and Mr Easter, were all school teachers. Auntie Edie seemed always to be ironing. It was not until years later that I learned she had to take in washing to make ends meet. It must have been a hard life, with every drop of water having to be drawn from the well. In winter the pump had to be thawed out with kettles of hot water before it would function. She used an iron with a deep base which opened to take a red-hot brick, pointed at one end: there were two bricks, one in the fire getting hot while the other was in the iron getting cold. Uncle Jim, formerly a farm worker but now very old, bent and almost toothless, would sit hunched over the fire, a pair of tongs in his hand, ready to effect the constant exchange of bricks. I remember him as a gentle old man, always with a ready smile.

In a field on the other side of the road lived Uncle Jim's youngest brother Isaac. He was a bachelor and lived in a converted railway carriage. It was a fascinating home to us children, with all the little rooms leading out of each other. He kept it scrupulously clean, but it smelled strongly of paraffin, his only means of heating, lighting, and cooking. (Many years later he knocked over one of his stoves and lost everything in the flames). I sensed that the grown-ups tended to be snobbish about Isaac, but we children loved him. He was a simple, almost child-like person himself and liked having us around him: he would always whittle sticks for us and put us wise on country matters. He kept chickens and had one belligerent rooster which behaved like a watchdog, challenging our entry vociferously, with flapping wings and pecking beak. I was afraid of it, much to Uncle Isaac's amusement. Auntie Edie had a cat similarly motivated: it would sit under the chair which stood by the kitchen door and jab out at our bare legs as we went in or out.

The first morning of the holiday, my first sight for almost twelve months of my beloved sand and sea, was one of uncontrollable excitement. It was not far down Beach Road to the dunes, and the gap where you could climb over on to the beach. Too impatient to wait for the others, I would run ahead and fling myself on to the sand, arms digging deep, as if I was trying to hug it to me. The gap was steep, but not so high as the dunes that rose on either side of it, and it was free of the sea holly and marram grass which covered them and which could cut you painfully if you did not tread carefully. There was one other way through the dunes. Beyond the handful of little cottages nestling on the land side of them, was a narrow passage, variously called Bog Alley or Paradise Lane, a noisome place, littered with tins, bottles and paper, probably the last resort of desperate holidaymakers. There were no public toilets in Palling.

At the top of the gap stood a little shop called Spion Kop, which sold refreshments and all the paraphernalia associated with holidays. A little beyond the shop, and at a lower level, was the lifeboat house. On the beach, above the water-line, were a few huts and a scattering of fishing boats. And that was all, except for the wide sweep of sun-bright golden sand: the heaving, limitless sea, and the glorious, invigorating air. That is a dangerous part of the coast: just where the land bends, it had unsuspected undercurrents and even small whirlpools. The passages of the currents can be seen when the tide goes out; it goes a long way out, leaving wide sandbanks, and between those banks and the shore are deep gullies filled with water. We called them 'lows': They were ideal for paddling and often deep enough in the centre for bathing. No-one familiar with the coast would attempt to bathe when the tide was going out. It was not unusual to hear of the death, or near death, of some hapless stranger. Even with the tide coming in it was impossible, in rough weather, to get beyond the breakers. I have seen strong men try, diving into the grey-green waves as they reared in, six feet high, cavernous and white-crested like huge, foam-flecked mouths, only to be spat out contemptuously on to the shingle that edged the sand until they gave up exhausted and smarting with gravel-rash.

When Father had collected the key from the old sailor who was renting us a hut, and we had established ourselves (other members of our party were in adjacent huts), the first business of the day was to visit *Spion Kop* for a bucket, spade and shrimp-net. I never knew what happened to those I had the year before. I was not allowed a metal spade in case I chopped my toes off. It was a grievance and an insult: the others had metal spades and in the matter of digging holes and building sand-castles their superiority over my blunt wooden one was manifest. There was a surprisingly similar age gap in the families of our party. My sister, who was ten years older than I, belonged with the group of older cousins and the Easters' first-born. I joined forces with my cousin Douglas and the younger Easter girl and we roped in any other child of similar age that might be around. I remember one miserable small boy whose insensitive parents had christened him Hagget. With the cruelty of children we called him Maggot. 'But Hagget's a family name,' he would protest tearfully. I think we were not the first to apply that sobriquet. The fishing boats drawn up behind the huts were favourite places for play. If you were bold enough you could traverse the length of a boat springing from plank seat to plank seat but, if you misjudged your distance, a fall into the bottom of the boat, where there were coils of thick rope, massive chains and metal boxes, could be painful.

The ladies normally sat on deck chairs and gossiped and knitted and made tea on a primus stove in the hut. The huts smelled of seaweed. They served to store the chairs and other belongings at night and, during the day, as changing rooms for bathers and as shelter from the rain. Not that there seemed to be much of that – or perhaps when one indulges in nostalgia one forgets the clouds.

The menfolk would play beach-bowls: the flat, wide sandbanks were ideal for it. They played with big rounded stones; grey-black flint with which the beach was strewn (and of which many of the oldest cottages were built). It was incredible that enough appropriate stones could be found. We children delighted in hunting for them. There were other attractive pebbles to be found too. Agates, carnelian and quartz, which Mr Easter could identify, and belemnite which he said was the fossilised bone of cuttlefish, many thousands of years old. From that small beginning grew my interest in rocks and gem craft.

Uncle Ernie was dying of consumption. I still remember the cold, clammy feel of his hands and lips when he kissed me goodbye at the end of his last holiday at Palling. On the way home he had to swerve to avoid two young cyclists who had overbalanced and fallen in the road in front of him: the car smashed into a lamp-post. No-one was seriously hurt, but the shock caused his condition to worsen rapidly and he died. Not long afterwards his elder daughter, who had taken the disease from him, also died and Douglas no longer came to Palling.

It is frequently preached that we should never go back, never try to recapture the past. I did go back to Palling, after a lapse of some forty years. Thankfully, I found that it had escaped the attention of developers, in fact it seemed smaller than before. The four cottages where Auntie Edie lived had been converted into two and given a face-lift which obscured the beautiful flint walls. There were no memories there. Spion Kop, the lifeboat house and the row of little cottages at the foot of the dunes had all gone, destroyed in the disastrous floods of 1953. There were no huts on the beach, but the tumultuous sea and the wide stretch of pale, pure gold sand were unchanged, unchangeable. I tried to people the beach with ghosts, but they would not come.

# *A Happy Thing*

If you asked me where it is I wouldn't be able to tell you, except that it is somewhere off the road between here and there. At least, it was three years ago. I was lost at the time, and several attempts to find it since have ended in frustration.

The placard was a roughly torn square of cardboard protected from the weather by a transparent plastic bag. It was fastened to the broken handle of a large garden fork by a piece of thick string. The fork was pushed into the ground in front of a hedge near a crazy wooden gate hanging on one hinge. Beyond the gate an overgrown path seemed to lead straight into a tangle of briars and bushes. The notice, in large uneven capitals, and written with black crayon, said simply "GRUB UTCH".

I was hungry. I was also foot-weary. I was considering whether this somewhat odd card could be interpreted as an invitation to rest and refreshment when a man appeared coming down the path. He was grinning and carrying a red balloon.

'Is there a café or restaurant or some such up there?' I asked him. 'You could say that,' he replied, and went off chuckling, the balloon bouncing about on its string above his head.

Since there would appear to be nothing lost by investigating, I started to walk up the path. Where it had seemed to run into a thicket it in fact turned sharply to the right. Here I nearly collided with a woman who was also carrying a balloon.

'The last time I came,' she said, 'it was a stick of liquorice. So good for you, you know.'

I watched her retreating figure, beginning to feel slightly bemused. As I turned back to continue up the path I met another man and another balloon.

'Don't tell me,' I said, 'the last time you came it was a stick of liquorice.'

'And the time before that,' he said, 'it was a packet of wildflower seeds, endangered species, you know, with instructions to plant them on a bank somewhere. I did it, too. Somehow what Miss Mary says do, you do.'

In another hundred yards the path ended at a gap in the hedge, and here the change in scenery was dramatic. No overgrown path, no tangled bushes and overhanging trees, but a large and beautifully kept garden with lawns, a sundial, a lily pond, and flower beds ablaze with colour. On the far side of the garden was a long, low house with thatched roof and diamond-paned windows. Wisteria clung to the walls and honeysuckle formed a thick porch over the doorway. The old oak door stood open. A crazy-paved path led in a wide arc from where I stood to the house.

There were three people in the garden; a man weeding one of the flower beds, another spraying some cordoned fruit trees against a far wall, and a lady dead-heading roses. I had to pass this lady on my way to the house.

'Wealthy eccentrics,' she said, 'must be.' I said nothing because there seemed nothing to say.

Pinned to the open door, above a huge, black, lion's-head knocker, was another notice also in black crayon on cardboard: this read, 'If you are in a hurry please do not come in.' I interpreted this to mean that service was slow. Well, they were honest about it, at any rate.

The tiny dim entrance hall smelled of lavender and furniture cream. There were bright rugs on the wooden floor which was black with age and polished to a deep shine. In the gloom at the back of the hall a faintly discernible staircase began its climb upwards but became lost in the shadows piled up under the low ceiling. On my left another open door led into an oak-panelled room where there were five or six white-clothed tables; two were occupied. I slid into a chair at the empty table near the door, and looked around. The floor was polished and rug-covered like the hall; there were old hunting prints on the walls and on shelves stood gleaming brass oil lamps and delicate china ornaments. Snowy, frilled lace curtains hung at the window.

'Menu, sir,' said a voice. A figure had materialised beside me, apparently from nowhere, though she must have come in soundlessly from the hall. I looked up to see an elderly lady who could have stepped straight out of an illustration in a Victorian magazine. Her black sateen dress was high necked, long sleeved, and reached to the floor. There was white lace frilling at neck and cuffs and she wore a lavender lace apron. Her white hair was piled on the top of her head and surmounted by a tiny white lace cap, threaded with a black velvet ribbon with ends which hung down the back. She was tall and slim with a peach-blossom complexion, and that she had been very handsome in her younger years was still evident.

She was so right for her setting. This I acknowledged after the first shock of surprise: a waitress in modern dress would have been an anachronism. I wondered if this could be Miss Mary, and almost immediately came confirmation when a voice from somewhere out of sight called 'Mary?' and my lady excused herself, saying that she would return very shortly and perhaps I would meanwhile care to be looking at the menu. I picked up the folded card she had left on the table and began to read with mounting bewilderment. Items were listed under the normal headings of Starters, Main Course, Sweets and Beverages but there normality ended. Under the first heading appeared Slush, Swill, and Blood-and-Bones; under the second, Botch-up, Cowpat, and Sea-scum. The sweets were Globules, Green Slime, and Poultice. No prices were quoted but by each heading a time was shown: 10 minutes against starters, 15 against main course, 10 against sweets and 5 against beverages. I took this to be an indication of waiting time, which clarified the notice on the front door. I was totally baffled by the menu and uneasy at the absence of prices. I never carried much money on my days rambling. Sensing that the man at an adjacent table was watching me, I looked up. He grinned.

'Your first time?' he asked and, when I nodded, 'I can recommend Blood-and-Bones, with Botch-up to follow.' He went on conversationally, 'There are two of them, you know, Miss Mary and Miss Elizabeth, twins, like as the proverbial peas. The only way to tell 'em apart is by their cap ribbons; Miss Elizabeth's is blue. They're both equally crazy.'

'No, Bert, the right word is unusual,' said his companion, whom I took to be his wife.

'Crazy,' repeated the man firmly, 'but whatever else she is, Miss Elizabeth is an angel because her cooking is out of this world.'

'Well, she's Cordon Bleu,' said his wife.

Cordon Bleu! My heart did a belly-flop and the change in my pocket suddenly felt woefully light. I decided discreet withdrawal was expedient, but it was too late; Miss Mary was back at my side, returning as silently as she had appeared the first time.

'So sorry to I had to leave you,' she said, 'are you ready to order now?' She had a gentle voice and a sweet, almost child-like face. Perhaps if I was short on the bill there wouldn't be any difficulty about arranging to send on the balance. Raising the sordid subject of money seemed somehow discourteous but I did venture, hesitantly, that I hoped I would have enough with me to pay.

'Oh, don't worry about it, dear boy,' said Miss Mary. 'Have a good meal. Energetic young people need to eat well.' I ordered and sat back to wait 10 minutes. Blood-and-Bones was on the table in under three; it turned out to be delicately spiced tomato soup with croutons.

The two at the next table were talking. 'I wonder what it will be this time,' said the woman, 'last time I planted crocus bulbs.'

'I hope it's not compost,' said Bert, 'I'm not good at compost.'

'Need you remind me,' said his wife feelingly, 'we were a fortnight getting the smell out of the car.'

I didn't see them leave. I was engrossed in the delights of the tenderest chicken on a bed of the whitest and fluffiest of rice, smothered with a mild but rich and thick curry sauce. For sweet I had chosen Green Slime without a qualm. It was lime mousse topped by thick cream and chopped walnuts, and was delicious. My guess that Bog Water would be coffee was correct. It was served black with cream in a little silver jug, and there was whiskey in it.

I was replete, relaxed, and very happy. Whatever the cost of the meal it was worth every penny. The fact that I would not have the requisite number of pennies had ceased to worry me.

Miss Mary materialised again and hoped I had enjoyed my meal. I said that I couldn't remember ever enjoying one so much, and to give my compliments to the cook. 'Oh, I'm so glad,' she said, and meant it; she glowed, 'Elizabeth will be *so* pleased.'

'Would you tell me,' I asked, 'what it all comes to?'

'It totals 40 minutes,' replied Miss Mary and as I stared uncomprehendingly, went on, 'I wonder if you would be so good as to come with me.' She led me to the back of the building, through a large kitchen where her exact counterpart (in blue-ribboned cap) was seated shelling peas. At her side, sharing that task, was the woman from the next table. In a paved yard Miss Mary indicated a pile of logs. 'I wonder it you would chop a few of those for us,' she asked, 'into kindling, you know. I thought perhaps you wouldn't mind one of the heavier jobs: you look a robust young man. Paid help is hard to get around here and not reliable when you do get it. Don't work too hard. Just a little will be a big help.' She had gone while I was still gathering my wits. I picked up a chopper and started on the logs. I caught myself smiling and realised I was enjoying myself. I wondered if Bert was knee-deep in compost and smiled more broadly.

In exactly 40 minutes Miss Mary was back. She exclaimed with delight at the pile of kindling, thanked me warmly, and ushered me back to the front of the house.

'I haven't paid yet, Miss Mary,' I reminded her.

'Oh, but you *have*, dear boy,' she replied. 'You have paid with your time. Time is more precious than money; time is life itself.' We were at the front door and she produced a balloon from the shadows behind it where I had not noticed them; a superior balloon, yellow with a face painted on it. '*Do* take a balloon,' she insisted, pressing the string into my hand, 'such *happy* things, balloons, I always think, don't you?'

By now I might have persuaded myself I dreamed it all. Only, I still have the balloon.

# *Ghosts Don't Smell*

The child sat at the end of the park bench swinging her feet. She had been skipping on the path round the pond but now the rope hung loosely between her legs. She gazed across the water, no longer enjoying – hardly noticing – the sparkling of the sunlight on the ripples and on the hoary grassy verges. Her mouth drooped at the corners. Presently she became aware that she was no longer alone; an elderly man was sitting at the other end of the bench. Catching her glance he nodded and smiled.

'Nice day,' he said. She regarded him gravely for a few moments. 'Never talk to strange men,' her gran was always telling her. Finally she said, 'Yes, for those who can enjoy it. When you have a lot of worries on your mind you don't have the heart to enjoy much.' He laughed. 'You're an old-fashioned little touch, I must say.'

She nodded. 'It's what comes of being brought up by an older generation, Gran says.'

'Ah, yes, no doubt,' he said. 'I'm sorry you have a lot of worries, but things do have a habit of working out, you know.'

She shook her head. After a silence and another considering look, she informed him, 'I'm Melissa and I'm ten.'

'Nice to meet you, Melissa,' he said. 'That's a pretty name – uncommon, too.'

'Yes, she nodded, 'there aren't any more Melissas in my class at school. There are two Claires and *three* Emmas. I don't know about the new school…' Her voice trailed away. Then, 'What's your name?' she asked.

'Silas.'

'Oh, that's uncommon too, isn't it? Are you very old?'

He laughed again, 'Pretty old, I guess. I stopped counting years ago.'

'Do you live near here?'

'Not now. I did once. Today I've just come back on business.'

'I live back there,' she jerked her head towards the row of houses behind them. 'I live with my gran, she's old, too. She's lovely. I saved her life, you know; that's what she always says. I didn't do it on purpose. I was only a baby. I was ill, you see, so we didn't go, or we'd have been killed too.'

'I see,' said the man, although it would have been surprising if he did.

Melissa nodded. 'It was a long time ago, of course. We lived in Scotland, my mummy and daddy and me, and Daddy's firm moved down here, so we came and stayed with Gran and Grandad while they looked for a house to move to. Well, they found one and were going to look at it this day when I was ill. I had a fever because I was teething or something. So Gran stayed home with me while Grandad drove Mummy and Daddy to see the house, only they never got there because a big lorry skidded and turned over on the car and they were all killed.'

'I'm so sorry,' said the man gently, 'what a terrible tragedy. And is it still making you unhappy?'

'Well, not really, I don't remember them, you see. Gran remembers Grandad, of course, and she misses him a lot. She says he was a wonderful person, which makes it so odd he didn't make a will for her. He died without making one: intestines they call it.'

'Intestate.'

'Oh.' She shot him a quick look to see if he was laughing at her; but his face was quite serious, only his eyes smiled, and it was a kind smile. 'Well – that. At least everybody *thought* he hadn't made one because there wasn't one anywhere, but it didn't matter because everything went to Gran anyway. But now a will has turned up and it's *awful* because we've got to lose *everything*.'

'Oh, dear, that is bad.'

'Shall I tell you about it? Gran says I talk too much.' But Melissa was clearly feeling a need to communicate and did not wait for his assent. She had wriggled a little closer. 'You see, Grandad was married before he married my gran. She was a widow with a son, this other wife, and he was horrid.' The man grunted feelingly, as if this was something he understood. 'Well, it didn't work out and Grandad got divorced and married Gran and they had my daddy. Now this other wife has died and the horrid son has found a will which Grandad made when he was married to her which leaves everything to her. *She* didn't know Grandad had died but *he* found out and he's taking *everything*.' Her face had flushed with indignation and distress.

'But your grandfather would have made out a later will, surely.'

'That's what Gran says. She says she's sure he would, but we can't find it.'

'Ask and it shall be given unto you, seek and ye shall find.'

'We've seeked everywhere,' the tone was faintly resentful, 'even in the loft. It's creepy up there. Lots of shadows making things look twice as big. But there's not much there: a couple of old chairs, and some china, and a case we take on holiday with our things in; that's empty, and two trunks that were Grandad's – he was in the Navy, you know – they have our winter curtains in the summer and the summer ones in the winter. We've got the winter ones up now; they're lovely dark red velvet, warm and cosy.'

'That was a quotation from the Bible,' said the man, 'Does your gran read the Bible?'

'I don't know.' Melissa was indifferent, her mind full of more important issues. 'Can he take the curtains, do you think? He's taking the house, and it's so nice there, looking out on the park. Gran says it's like a big front garden. Grandad grew roses in it and, do you know, they're still there, after all these years. *He'll* get them, of course, with the house. Gran will hate that.' Her voice was bitter. 'Gran says the Council will find us a flat on the Estate, but it's dreadful there. We went to have a look. It's a long way: we had to take two buses, and it's awful. Lots of great square blocks and no gardens, and washing hanging out of the windows and dirty children running around screaming, and loud music, and men hanging around all the corners smoking, or sitting on the ground drinking out of cans. Gran says she'll never be able to let me out on my own. I'll have to go to a new school because the one I go to is too far away. All my friends are there. But worstest of all, we've got to get rid of Fluffy because the flats don't let you have pets.' Her voice had become tremulous with tears. 'I've had her since she was a baby kitten and she's beautiful, with big yellow eyes. She sleeps on my bed. Gran says it's not right, but she doesn't stop her.' She fell silent. It was all said.

'That's a very heavy weight of trouble for such young shoulders,' the man said gently.

She sat staring, unseeing at the bright red handles of her skipping rope. Finally she looked up saying, with a trace of embarrassment, 'I do run on, don't I, like Gran says.'

'No, no,' he said, 'it often helps to talk about things.'

She smiled suddenly, the whole of her little face lighting up.

'You're nice,' she said, 'Will you be here another day?'

'I'm afraid not. I go back tonight. But I'll be thinking about you my dear, and hoping things get better for you. Perhaps you should be getting home, it's chilly now the sun's gone.'

'I expect it's nearly tea time,' Melissa agreed. 'Gran will be looking for me.' She slid off the seat. 'Good-bye then.' She gave him another smile and made her way up the path to the gate. When she reached it she turned to wave to her new friend, but he had already gone.

'I was just coming to call you,' said Gran when she let her in. 'It's too cold to be sitting around on park seats.'

'That's what the man said,' said Melissa.

'What man?' Gran's voice was sharp. 'How often do I have to warn you about talking to strange men?'

'He was sitting on the seat with me and he spoke first. It would have been rude not to answer him.'

'You can't be too careful. I didn't see him or I'd have been out to bring you in.'

'Oh, he was all right, Gran. He was old and kind. He didn't offer me sweets, or anything. I told him all about the will and everything. He said he's sure Grandad made a new one.'

'Then perhaps he'd like to tell us where to find it,' said Gran tartly. 'Melissa, must you discuss our private business with any stranger you meet!'

'Well, he wasn't really anyone,' said the child, 'He was a ghost.'

'Oh, really, Melissa. These fantasies of yours are going to get you into trouble one of these days. People who don't know you will think you tell lies.'

'But I'm sure he was a ghost, Gran, and you didn't see him, which proves it. Ghosts can only be seen by people they want to be seen by.'

'I didn't see him,' said Gran defensively, 'because I wasn't looking all the time you were out, that's all.'

'Besides,' Melissa persisted, 'he didn't smell.'

'He didn't what!'

'He didn't smell. Everybody smells, you know, Gran,' said Melissa with all the wisdom of her ten years, 'nice or nasty. People smell of scent, or sweat, or garlic, or cigarette smoke, or shoe polish. Babies smell of sick, Mrs Baker smells as if she's just been taken out of mothballs.' She giggled. 'And Joe from the corner smells of petrol even when he's wearing his Sunday best. But ghosts can't smell because they're not real people.'

'Well I declare,' said Gran, for once in her life at a loss for words, 'and what do I smell of Miss, if you please?'

'Oh,' Melissa beamed, 'all warm and soapy except when you've been using bleach. I hate the smell of bleach.'

Gran shook her head, half amused, half amazed at her grand-daughter's perceptiveness. 'Well, come and get your tea,' she said. 'Pull the curtains for me, there's a dear, while I pour out.'

Melissa drew the red velvet curtains across the windows, fingering the soft, rich fabric lovingly. The winter dusk was already passing into night. The park was a smudge of dark shadows, a faint glimmer showing where the pond lay. Melissa loved to watch that glimmer turn into a white gleam when the moon came up. There would be nothing to see from the flats but other flats. She turned slowly back into the room and took her seat at the table. But, never quiet for long, she returned to her encounter with the stranger.

'He said, "Ask and it shall be given unto you, seek and ye shall find.' It's a quotation from the Bible, he said.'

'So it is,' grunted Gran.

'He might have been a vicar, or something once. He said did you read the Bible.'

'What's it got to do with him, I'd like to know,' Gran bristled. 'What did you tell him?'

'I said I didn't know. Do you, Gran?'

'When you've had the troubles in life that I've had,' said Gran, not giving a direct answer, 'it tends to put you off religion.'

Melissa helped herself to bread and butter and went on prattling. 'He said Melissa was a pretty name and an uncommon one.'

'So it is,' said Gran. 'No doubt you asked him his name.' The sarcasm was lost on Melissa.

'Oh yes. He said it was Silas. That's an uncommon name too, isn't it Gran? I like it. When I grow up and get married and have a little boy, I think I'll call him Silas.'

Gran had suddenly become quite still, her teacup in her hand, her eyes fixed on her granddaughter. Slowly she put the cup down. 'I hope you will,' she said quietly. Still slowly, she got up from the table and crossed to one of the alcoves by the fireplace. Its shelves were full of books and an assortment of oddments. On the bottom shelf, under a jumble of gramophone records and old magazines was a large, leather-bound volume with brass corners and clasp.

She pulled it out with some difficulty and carried it back to the table, watched by a now silent Melissa. In faded gold leaf on the heavily embossed cover were the words Holy Bible. Gran unfastened the clasp and raised the cover. Underneath was a double sheet of thick grey foolscap: it was headed 'The Last Will and Testament of me, Silas John McAllister'...

# *Waterspell*

He had left his shoes and socks somewhere under the cliff and rolled up the legs of his trousers. He danced along the edge of the waves like a child, delighting in the rush of the cool water between his toes, the pull of the sand beneath his feet as each wave receded. He stamped along the skeins of spindrift left festooning the beach, laughing at the puff-balls of rainbow-coloured suds he sent flying. He was utterly and completely happy.

Jonathan had never before seen the sea. There are possibly few young adults of whom that could be said; but, when your mother has been a widow for most of your life, and there has never been much money around, and you live a long, long way from the coast, seaside holidays just don't happen.

Which, in Jonathan's case, amounted to deprivation because he had a passion for water. It was something he had been born with. Where other babies might object to being put into a bath, Jonathan objected to being taken out, leaning back over his mother's arm and trying to snatch up a handful of water to take out with him. And he had been known, as a toddler, to clamber back into the bath after he had been dried and dressed. He would watch, absorbed, the long straight flow from a tap and the whirlpool it created plunging into water in a bowl. Rain drew him out of doors by invisible strings and he would stand with upturned face until he was drenched. He would stand astride rain-filled gutters watching the racing water, pleated into its narrow confines, tumbling over obstacles and rushing, gurgling, down gratings into the dark, mysterious river below. He would kneel beside puddles staring at his reflection: and whenever Jonathan was missing he could usually be found sitting by the pond in the nearby park, laughing at the spreading circles round goldfish rising to the surface.

Preoccupation with water was not his only peculiarity, although it was the most marked. He was a pretty boy, with glossy dark hair and a sweet smile, gentle and affectionate. Only his eyes tended to see into a world different from the one around him.

They could do little with him at school. When he was twenty he was taken into a psychiatric unit, but they could do little with him there either, so, after eight months, they discharged him. He was not schizophrenic, he certainly had no tendency towards violence. He was simply fey. There was, of course, this strange obsession with water, but that was harmless. So they sent him home.

But home was not where it had been. During the time that he was away his mother had met and married Percy and moved with him to a bungalow near the coast. It was there that Jonathan joined her; an arrangement which did not particularly commend itself to Percy.

So now Jonathan had been introduced to the sea. He had stood spellbound on the cliff-top, staring open-mouthed at an expanse of water greater than anything in the realms of his imagination. It stretched away and away, beyond the limit of his sight; a glinting, glittering deep metallic blue. With a cry of pure ecstasy he left his companion and went rushing and leaping down the steep path into the cove below.

To Jonathan every wave was a miracle-worker, turning the pale dry sand to amber and the pebbles into gems. The sweeping forward and drawing back made strange music. With the incoming tide he moved higher and higher up the beach, until there was only a narrow strip of sand between the waves and the sheer face of the cliff. Then that too, was covered, and the water was round his ankles: in only minutes it had risen to his knees. Jonathan wriggled his pale toes, watching with amusement little spurts of sand eddy up between them. When the water was above his knees his feet were lost in a liquid darkness. How lovely the water was, so soft and with the sheen of velvet. He tried to stroke it but the ripples tripped over his fingers. The swell was now making it difficult for him to keep his balance and the waves were throwing him back against the rock. He began to feel the first stirrings of anxiety. He looked in front and to both sides, and there was nothing to see but water. Behind was the rock face, the only accessible part of the path that he had raced down was now submerged. He felt suddenly lonely.

For all his lifelong preoccupation with water Jonathan had never learned to swim. While he was at school there had been the usual sessions at the baths, but he could never be prevailed upon to do anything other than stand in the shallow end peering down at his feet, or scooping up hands full of water to watch it trickle through his fingers.

The strengthening surge of the tide dragged Jonathan away from the cliff then flung him back against it. He whimpered in protest. Then, out beyond the entrance to the cove, a wave began to build up, growing in size as it rolled in, dwarfing the waves around it. A very king among breakers it reared its head, crowned with spray, and swept majestically and seemingly with purpose, directly towards Jonathan. He watched, mesmerised as it towered above him: then it crashed down, its huge foam-flecked mouth snatching Jonathan up, turning him over and then spitting him out viciously against the rock. Its violence expended, it then slid along the cliff and the sea was calm again. The last thing Jonathan was conscious of was water, now soothing and gentle, caressing his torn and broken head.

Strolling back to the cliff's edge some fifteen minutes later, Percy peered over at the sea churning below. He saw what looked like one of Jonathan's white trainers bobbing to and fro with the swell. It might almost, he thought as he moved on, be regarded as the perfect murder.

# *The Outing*

'Will she be all right here, do you think?' asked one of the women. 'It's nicely out of the wind.' They had dragged the chair through soft sand and wedged it against a breakwater.

'Oh yes,' said the other, 'the wheels have sunk right into the sand; it can't move. Here, this will make quite sure of it.' She unearthed a broken half brick and pushed it down in front of a wheel.

'You'll be all right, lovey,' said the first woman to Martha, tucking the rug more closely around her knees, 'we won't be long.'

'Ah,' said Martha, and gave her a snaggle-toothed smile.

They moved away down the beach, glancing back once or twice. 'We're not going out of sight; we can keep an eye on her. They sleep a lot at that age. I do believe she's asleep already.'

'Oh, Martha's no trouble. We wouldn't normally bring anyone of her age, of course, but Grace couldn't come without, and she can do with a break.'

At the water's edge they joined others of their group, took off their shoes, tucked their skirt hems into their knicker legs and paddled, splashing like children, revelling in the wash of cold water over their hot feet. The sand was burning under a cloudless sun.

Martha was not asleep. She had only closed her eyes briefly against the sun's glare. She was not tired. She had slept most of the way down. She had been lifted into the coach and put in a seat behind the driver, where she could see very little. The chair had gone into the luggage compartment at the back. It was boring, so she had slept, but she had no wish to sleep now: there was too much to see. Martha had never before been to the sea. When you live in the heart of England the sea is a long way away. She would not be here now, but for the kindness of the women. They were all late-middle-aged, members of the Mother's Union of St. Joseph's Church, and she was not one of them. This was their annual day's outing to the coast, and it had been good of them to bring her. Now the women were intent on enjoying themselves. They had already had ice-creams. Martha had not managed hers very well: her hands were not always responsive to her will. It was galling. There would be sandwiches later, which should be less of a problem.

Martha's enjoyment was in everything she saw. She gazed around, entranced by this magical new world. At the top of the beach, where she was sitting, just below the promenade, and which was reached only by the seas of winter storms, the sand was grey and grubby and litter strewn. Martha did not notice it. Lower down it was a brilliant gold, and the sea was like dark blue velvet studded with diamonds. The sky too, was deep blue, an unbroken expanse stretching away and away for ever. Because in the distant haze there was no visible meeting of sky and sea, the sky seemed limitless. Martha had never seen so much sky, and she could hardly take her eyes from the wonder of it. At home the sky was small; just little patches between roofs and tall chimneys, and never this peerless blue.

A young woman dragged a baby's pram across the sand and parked it near Martha's chair, and moved a few yards away to sit on the sand. In the pram was a belligerent-looking infant. Martha smiled at him but was treated to a scowl in return. Her gaze was drawn back to the beach, where so much was happening. There seemed to be children everywhere, digging, building sand-castles, chasing big coloured balls, dashing in and out of the waves accompanied by excited dogs. There was a small girl with a big red balloon on a string, and a boy with a kite which had a too-short tail: it zoomed and bucked, dipped, twisted and nose dived.

The belligerent-looking infant was amusing himself by removing everything removable from his pram. Out went the rattle, teething ring, rag-book, teddy bear, rug, pillow, plastic cup and one shoe which he had managed to wriggle out of. When nothing else was left he tried to remove himself, but was frustrated in that endeavour by a secure harness. He raised a loud and piercing complaint, bringing his mother to the pram, scolding and soothing. She restored all the discarded items and replaced the shoe, then went back to her seat on the sand; whereupon the infant embarked on a repeat performance.

The first Martha had found amusing, but the second time round it was rather tedious. The mother apparently thought so too and, unstrapping the infant, took him to sit beside her on the beach, where he promptly sampled the sand to assess its food potential. Finding it had none he again resorted to vociferous protest.

Meanwhile, lower down the beach, there was high drama; the little girl had let go of her balloon. It soared up and up into the sky and out to sea, never deviating from its course, watched with some envy by the boy with the recalcitrant kite. Finally the eye could follow its path no longer and it dissolved into the brightness. The little girl was inconsolable and was at length led away by an adult, to return a little while later with a replacement balloon, secured firmly to her wrist.

A little way out from the water's edge, beyond where the women were paddling, were three wind-surfers: one had a bright yellow sail, one a red and one white. Martha was engrossed by them. They were not expert surfers: if they had been they would have been far less entertaining. But they could not handle their sails, which spent more time flat than upright; they did not know how to deal with the frolicsome wind, and were up and down like Jack-in-the-boxes. They were also too close together, so that on the few occasions when all three were upright at the same time they inevitably collided and all ditched together with a concerted splash. This delighted Martha. She laughed aloud and slapped her hands on her knees.

The women were straggling up from the water's edge, one after the other. It was time for lunch. Martha beamed at them, her eyes sparkling with the joy of it all. Her woollen cap had slipped to a rakish angle over one ear, allowing a few wisps of no-colour hair to escape. They came and fussed over her, straightening the cap, smoothing and tucking in the rug, which didn't need it.

'Are you all right, lovey? Enjoying it?' asked one of the women who had settled the chair on the sand.

'Why look at her,' said another, 'I do declare the sky is in her eyes. I never saw such blue eyes.'

Martha laughed, crinkling those eyes at the corners. 'Ah,' she said; then suddenly throwing out both arms on a gesture as if she would like to gather in to herself all this beauty, this wonderful experience, she added, 'baa, blah, boo.'

It was inadequate to express her feelings, but what more could be expected from someone barely twelve months old.

# *Watchdog*

Jake had been Miss Faulkner's odd job man for a number of years. He was lazy and workshy and had never held down a regular job, but 'doing' for Miss Faulkner was easy; he could take his time (and did) and she paid well. If she knew of his reputation in the village of being a petty crook she gave no sign of it.

Miss Faulkner lived in an isolated house about a mile from the village with just a dog for company. She was elderly and, although still spry, could no longer manage jobs around the house nor the heavier gardening: so Jake repaired fences, unblocked drains, mowed the lawn, patched worn lino, and made himself generally useful. She was appreciative and kind. But the dog didn't like him.

Bruce was an ugly bull-mastiff/alsatian cross with powerful jaws and an evil glint in his eyes when he was looking at Jake, hardly letting him out of his sight and, whenever their eyes met, he snarled. As if that were not enough, there was a coloured photograph of him in a frame on the hall windowsill: the eyes were uncannily alive and those eyes, too, seemed to follow Jake around whenever he was in the hall.

'I can't understand it,' Miss Faulkner said, 'he's usually so friendly. Perhaps there's some kind of smell about you. I haven't noticed it myself, but dogs are sensitive to such things.' She adored the dog, he was her companion, friend and protector, but Jake hated and feared him: if there was any smell attaching to Jake it was engendered by those emotions. Attempts to win Bruce over by offerings of chocolate or dog treats were fruitless; the gifts were ignored.

Miss Faulkner's house resembled a high-class junk shop. It was cluttered from wall to wall with a wide assortment of articles, either inherited or collected during a long lifetime. There were pictures and photographs, tapestries and small pieces of antique furniture, crystal, silverware, bronze figurines, Chinese vases and bowls, porcelain ornaments and decorated clocks. Jake coveted them; not for themselves – the nearest Jake came to appreciating beauty was in the winking colours in the froth on his beer – but for what they represented in terms of cash value. There must have been a small fortune crammed into those rooms and he was sure that, with so much overcrowding, Miss Faulkner would not miss the odd item purloined from time to time. The difficulty was not in taking things but in getting them out of the house. There was nothing small enough to slip into a pocket and any bulge inside his jacket would be noticed. Old she might be, but Miss Faulkner was still eagle-eyed. And there was Bruce: that uncanny brute would be bound to know he was carrying out something which didn't belong to him. He shuddered at the thought of those jaws savaging his legs. So he took no chances. It would, in any case, be foolish to queer his pitch. The old lady was a useful source of easy income. She couldn't live all that much longer and, so far as anyone knew, she had no relatives. If he played his cards right she might even remember him in her will and, anyway, once the coast was clear he could take his pickings without any trouble. So he bided his time, more or less resignedly: until he suddenly found himself in urgent need of money.

Jake was caught riding a stolen motor-bike without insurance or licence and fined. The alternative to the fine was jail. Jake had some experience of jail and he didn't care for it. But he could not pay the fine. What a fool he'd been. If he'd flogged the damn bike straight away he wouldn't have been caught with it. He brooded on his predicament, his thoughts inevitably turning to the wealth up at 'the house', just waiting to be tapped. It would be dead easy if it wasn't for the dog. There was only one thing for it, the dog would have to go. Bruce had a weakness for raw liver. A generous helping of raw liver, laced with weed killer and left in the garden where he could find it, easily should do the trick.

It did. Miss Faulkner came down one morning to find Bruce pathetically hunched up and quite dead. She was heartbroken.

The matter was talked about in the Ploughman's Arms that evening. Jake was propping up the bar on his own, as was usual. He was not popular in the local pub; he was not a sociable man, had never been known to stand anyone a pint, so he was left to drink alone. He was staring into his fifth beer when Micky Collins, who was sitting at a nearby table with three cronies, said 'I hear old lady Faulkner, up at the house, have lost 'er dog.'

'Aye,' said Bill Smithers, 'poisoned, they say. Seems a rum do. Dunno how 'un could've got hold of it.'

'One of the farms p'raps, after getting foxes – or rabbits.'

'Dunno none as 'd do it that way.'

'Old lady's fair cut up. Thought the world of 'un, she did.'

Jake felt a faint twinge of conscience about Miss Faulkner; she was a nice old girl. But he had no compunction whatever over the dog, hateful creature: he'd only got what was coming to him.

'She'll be lost without 'un,' this from Jerry Lomax. 'Taint safe, neither, up there all on 'er own. It's a lonely place. She needs a good guard dog.'

'Mebbe she'll get another,' said Micky, 'best if 'er did, sooner the better. My cousin might know of one. I'll ask 'un.'

Jake's thoughts were pulled up sharp. He hadn't thought about Miss Faulkner getting another dog. But she might, she might just do that. There wasn't time to let the grass grow under his feet.

Dr. Sheppard passed Jake on his way out of the pub with two friends. 'Go easy on that stuff, Jake,' he warned, 'I've told you before. You drink too much. Bad for the heart.'

'Not for his,' said Bill, 'doubt if he's got one.' The others chortled and Jake scowled. He downed his sixth pint and left. There was work to be done.

---

In the early hours of the next morning Miss Faulkner was awakened by the sound of furious barking followed by a shrill scream and a thud. She struggled up in bed trying to clear her head of the mists of sleep. All was quiet. Had she really heard something or was it part of a dream? She had to own to some feelings of nervousness without Bruce around: she was very vulnerable in this isolated place. She would have to get another dog, she supposed, though nothing could replace her beloved Bruce; there had been such deep understanding between them. She felt the tears rising again but forced them down: crying would not bring him back. After a few moments she got out of bed. She would have to go down and take a look round. Although there was no sound in the house she knew she would not be able to rest again without first checking that everything was as it should be. So, putting on her dressing-gown and slippers, she went downstairs.

The back door to the conservatory was open and on the floor lay the body of a man. Miss Faulkner recognised him at once, although his face was contorted; the short red beard with the untidy dark hair could only belong to Jake. (It was odd, she had often thought, that a dark-haired man should have a ginger beard.) He was clearly dead. His eyes were wide open and fixed in a look of horror. His mouth, too, was open and with one hand he was clutching his throat as a man might who was choking. Miss Faulkner did not touch him; she was a detective-fiction addict and knew that evidence should not be interfered with. She went to the telephone and called the police.

They came and brought Dr. Sheppard and an ambulance with them. Dr. Sheppard examined the body while the police questioned Miss Faulkner. She could tell them very little. She had come down because she thought a noise had awakened her and that was what she had found. Jake was put in the ambulance and the police left. Dr. Sheppard stayed for a few minutes.

'Are you all right, my dear?' he asked. 'A nasty experience. I can give you something for shock.'

'No thank you, I'm quite all right,' said Miss Faulkner, 'I shall make myself a nice strong cup of tea. Can I offer you one?'

'Love one, but I daren't stop. Expecting a call to Jenny Firth any minute, her baby's on the way.'

'You say it was a heart attack?' Miss Faulkner was not interested in Jenny Firth. Jenny had six children already, all looking like ragamuffins, and adding to her family was highly irresponsible.

'Not much doubt about it, but he'll be looked at again at the hospital. Seems to have suffered some sort of shock, or fright. But he was a typical heart potential; lazy, overweight, drank too much, smoked too much. I was always warning him. Odd about the tooth marks. You don't have another dog, do you?'

'No.'

'And there aren't any big dogs hereabouts?'

'Not to my knowledge. Why?'

'He was clutching his throat – you must have noticed – and when I moved his hand away there were tooth marks on his throat; quite deep, although they hadn't penetrated the skin. Recent, too; they hadn't begun to flatten out and bruising hadn't started.'

'Perhaps a fox..?'

'Foxes don't spring at people's throats and their jaws are too small and teeth too sharp to have made those marks. Well, I'd better be on my way if you're sure you're alright.'

Miss Faulkner assured him that she was.

'Certainly puzzling, those tooth marks,' he said as she let him out. Miss Faulkner closed the front door and stood gazing thoughtfully at Bruce's photograph on the windowsill. Those wonderfully alive eyes seemed to gaze straight back at her with a meaningful look. She nodded at the portrait and smiled.

# Lust

Lola served in the Italian wine bar. She was a highly-coloured lady of indeterminate age: red-cheeked, black-haired, with flashing dark eyes that were slightly protuberant, and thick, sensuous lips. Her chin rested on the cushion of its double, which padded her neck round to her ears. Her ample bosom, assisted by an up-lift bra, projected aggressively: she might almost have rested her tray on it. To ensure the needful balance, nature had endowed her with a generously proportioned bottom, which arched away from her waist like a bustle. Whether you were in front of her or behind, you were at risk from assault.

'Ooh, la la,' said the men, an observation more usually associated with a French bistro. The women looked down their noses.

'Voluptuous,' drooled Malcolm.

'Vulgar,' snapped Gill.

But the women's disquiet at their menfolk's seduction was needless: Lola responded to lascivious glances and suggestive overtures with indifference.

At the end of her shift, Lola left by the back entrance and walked the short distance to her apartment. Once inside, she slumped into an easy chair and put her feet up to rest her aching legs. How she despised those oily, ogling men with their surreptitiously groping hands! She opened the box from the patisserie that she had brought in with her and allowed her eyes to lust over its contents, while she fed chocolate drops to an overweight cat. This was seduction. This absorption in anticipation almost rivalled the transitory bliss of realisation. Like other pleasures, once taken, they were gone. To contemplate the succulent delicacies, oozing their fresh cream, to tantalise herself with indecision over which to eat first, brought complete sensual satisfaction. This (frequent) indulgence was, she knew, a form of self-love; but that, in her experience, was the only love that was constant.

# *The Last Leaf*

The atmosphere at breakfast in the servants' hall was sombre. Voices, when there was any conversation at all, were low. The child sat big-eyed and silent, her porridge almost untouched; apprehension made her stomach fluttery. She sensed that something was seriously amiss without knowing what. She was a thin child and small for her age. Her brown hair hung in two plaits down her back, tied with black ribbon. She wore a starched white cotton pinafore over her long-sleeved brown dress, and well darned brown woollen stockings: the pinafore had goffered broderie-anglais over the shoulders and round the hem. Her feet, in black patent shoes with buckles, were hooked tightly round the legs of her chair. Her hands fidgeted nervously in her lap.

There were five persons at the scrubbed wooden table, besides the child. There was her father Bert, coachman and groom; her mother Florrie, parlourmaid; Bill the gardener and his nephew, a lad named William who was second gardener and general handyman; and Cook. It is to be presumed that Cook had another name but the child had never heard her called anything but Cook. Her mother and Cook also wore bibbed white pinafores over their brown dresses. Until recently the establishment had included a Mr. and Mrs. Forbes, butler and housekeeper, but they had left. 'They felt the chill in the wind,' the child's father had said. They had not been replaced. It was a long time since the Mistress had left her room for more than an hour or two at a time, and they were not needed. There was also Sarah, the Mistress's personal maid and companion, but she usually took her meals with the Mistress.

After what had seemed a long silence Bert said, 'When the last leaf falls winter has come.' He was sometimes given to fanciful phrases.

'Will you be all right, Bill?' asked Florrie.

'My sister, William here's ma, has offered for me to stay with her till I find somewhere,' said Bill, ' How about you?'

Florrie shook her head. 'It's not easy with a child,' she said, 'we were lucky to get here.'

'I've been spoke for,' said Cook somewhat smugly.

The exchange meant little to the child, but did nothing to raise her spirits. Whatever the trouble was it had started, she felt sure, with the arrival the previous day of the three gentlemen who had spent so long in the Mistress's room. One, a portly bushy-whiskered gentleman in frock coat and gaiters, she had heard addressed deferentially as 'doctor.' They had left eventually and then returned in the evening with a young woman named Biddie whom they called a nurse. They had left again but Biddie had stayed in the old lady's room overnight. This morning the men had come back.

'Emmie,' said her mother, 'If you've had all you want, go and see to the drawing-room fire, and mind not to spill any ashes.' The child slipped from her chair and went to do her mother's bidding. She loved the pretty drawing room, as indeed she loved all of the gracefully appointed rooms in the old manor, with their beautiful, ornate ceilings. And she loved the gardens outside the house, the smooth lawn and bright flower beds so caringly tended by Bill, and the little twisted stream at its foot; and beyond that and the great old trees was the ornamental pond where there were ducks to be fed, and where sea-gulls sought shelter in winter. She had come here as little more than a baby, nine years before, and to her it was home; she had known no other. But, now, she was dimly aware of a threat to her security.

The drawing room was kept cheerful and bright although the Mistress never came here now. At one time she had spent most of her days in the charming room she preferred to all the others or, if the weather was clement, she would sit on the balcony outside the long window. She would sit either dozing or gazing across the park; her eyes, dim and hooded, perhaps seeing little of the present but peopling the grounds with loved ones from the past, when the house was alive with young voices. The flowers of the family had faded, one by one, and she was the last withered leaf which had defied the autumn winds. To Emmie she had always been a remote figure, in her black bombazine and white lace cap. She was very old, like the Queen was old. She looked exactly how Emmie imagined the Queen to look; she had never seen the Queen. Whether the old lady was aware of Emmie the child did not know. She bobbed a quick curtsy whenever she scurried past on an errand, but received no recognition.

Back in the kitchen she said hesitantly: 'Mama, is the Mistress ill?'

'Failing,' said her mother, 'and when she goes we all go. The Council won't want us here.'

'You mean go away from here?' Emmie was aghast, ' but this is our home.'

'Not our own home, you foolish child,' said her mother, ' we're only servants here as well you know.'

'But… but where will we go?'

'God knows,' said her mother on a sigh, 'God alone knows.' She turned away, brushing a hand across her eyes.

After a few moments of stunned inaction the child wandered out into the grounds, where she found William trimming a hedge. She watched him in silence, wriggling the toe of each shoe in turn against its partner, as she stood first on one foot and then the other. Finally she said timidly, 'William, the Mistress isn't dead, is she?' It was a plea for reassurance.

'Nigh on, I shouldn't wonder,' said William, 'she's a mighty great age, you know. Ninety-five, they tell me. That's older than the Queen. People don't live for ever.'

Emmie's mouth drooped. ' What's the Council, William?'

'Dunno, rightly,' said William, 'but they get this place when the old lady goes and we'll all be out on our ears.'

The child's lower lip quivered and tears pricked the back of her eyelids.

'Emmie!' It was her mother's voice. 'Emmeline!' She turned and ran back to the house.

'Take this tray up to the gentlemen,' said her mother, 'and mind you carry it careful. And ask Miss Sarah if the fire needs attention. And make sure to knock before you go in.'

Emmie took the heavy silver tray and started carefully up the stairs, pausing on each step. On the tray were glasses and a bowl of steaming punch, and a plate of biscuits. The biscuits were one of Cook's specialities, thin, crisp, dark brown and shiny. The sight of them made Emmie's mouth water and she was beginning to have regrets about her missed breakfast. She wondered if one biscuit would be missed if she slipped it into her pinafore pocket. The difficulty attending that small deceit was that to perform it she needed a free hand. She would have to put the tray down, of course, before she could knock on the door; and that, said temptation, would be her opportunity. But as she stooped to place the tray on the floor outside the Mistress's room, the door was opened. Emmie straightened slowly, her eyes travelling up gaitered legs and coming to rest on a heavy gold Albert stretched across an ample waistcoat. She shot a frightened glance up at the whiskered face as the tray was taken from her, certain that her intention had been divined, but the doctor dismissed her with a nod and closed the door behind him. She was too timid to knock and ask about the fire.

The day was a strange one: the gentlemen went and came, and normal routine was disrupted. Emmie wandered through the house, unhappy, unsettled and, for most of the time, forgotten by the grown-ups. Finally, when it was growing dusk, the gentlemen came downstairs and called for their carriages. The domestics clustered behind them on the manor steps and Emmie, while keeping out of sight, crept close enough to listen.

'Nanny Smith will be along shortly to help Biddie lay her out,' the whiskered gentleman was saying, 'I've already put her on call.'

'And I will arrange with the undertaker,' said one of the other men, 'there's nothing for you to worry about.'

Emmie watched as the carriages rolled away, the clatter of horses hoofs fading into the distance. The servants withdrew into the house and the door was closed. There was no family left to mourn the old lady, but a child in the shrubbery wept.

# *Cast a Long Shadow*

Alfred Potts looked what he was, every inch the retired Civil Servant, one of the old school, a fast disappearing breed from the days when the Service was a highly regarded and respected institution and its members conducted themselves soberly in both dress and behaviour. Alfred Potts was, by nature, eminently suited to his calling: efficient, precise, upright – a little humourless perhaps in preserving his dignity – and intensely loyal to his Department. Even among his contemporaries he was never a man to be treated familiarly – he was never Alf, nor Fred, nor Potts. To his subordinates he was Mr. Potts or Sir: to his peers and superiors he was Alfred. Among the annual intake of disrespectful youth he was sometimes referred to as 'Old Potty', but never within earshot. He was respected because he merited respect and he was secure in that knowledge; it never crossed his mind that it could have been otherwise.

Since his retirement Alfred had gone to live with his widowed sister. Alfred had never married. The gentle barbs from the god of the divine passion had never tried to penetrate his dry exterior. Had they done so he would have retreated in alarm; such an intrusion into his well-regulated life would have been disturbing and unwelcome. His sister lived in a bungalow in a pretty area just outside London where suburbia began to rub shoulders with country. Alfred liked the country but he made no concessions to it in the matter of dress. Every morning, precisely at ten, he went for a walk dressed in his black coat and pinstripes and – subject to the season – his grey Burberry, and wearing his bowler hat. But for the absence of a briefcase he could have been going to a meeting at the Cabinet Office. Routine was essential to Alfred, he would have been lost and unhappy without it. He could not turn his back on forty years of disciplined living. The morning walk was an extension of the walk he had made every weekday of his working life, from Green Park Station across St. James's Park to his office.

It was a fine April morning when Alfred prepared for his walk.

The clean-washed sky was thin blue with a scattering of dimpled white cloud. The sun was warm and Alfred decided against his Burberry but in favour of his umbrella, April being traditionally the month of showers. His elderly transistor had that morning wheezed asthmatically for a few minutes and then choked itself into silence, so he had not been able to listen to the news and weather forecast as was his habit: an enforced and irritating break in routine. His sister never bothered with the radio before midday. So, rather than take any chances, he took his umbrella. Alfred disliked getting wet. He also disliked his umbrella: it had embarrassing associations and its existence kept evergreen memories of an incident he would have been thankful to forget. Unfortunately the umbrella had been a gift from his sister and discarding it in favour of another would have required him to give an explanation, and the matter was one he preferred to keep to himself. He had contemplated losing the umbrella, but Alfred was a transparently honest person and would have found it impossible to sustain a deceit. Moreover, his name was engraved on the silver band round the handle and some well-meaning busybody would have been sure to return it to him.

The umbrella had a long, thin, ferrule, unusually sharp at the point. He could spear scraps of paper with it on the grass verges. Alfred liked spearing scraps of paper because litter offended him. But he had no desire to spear anything else, and he had been forced to recognise the umbrella as a potentially dangerous weapon. Even now, after the lapse of some eleven years, he grew hot and unhappy at the recollection of that little scene on the bus in the Strand. Umbrella over his arm, he had left his seat to stand in the gangway with other passengers waiting to alight at the approaching stop when, without warning, the bus swerved violently, throwing those standing off balance. They pitched into each other and on top of people still seated, hands shooting out wildly to grab backs of seats and handrails. The arm Alfred flung out to save himself was the one on which his umbrella was hooked and the pointed end, out of his control, tore a hole in the nylons of a seated lady. The lady was not amused and made that verbally evident. In spite of the expensive elegance of her outfit and her Mayfair accent she was not too well bred to create a scene. Alfred could hardly be held to blame, nor for that matter, could the bus driver. The culprit was a jay-walker who would have been under the wheels of a taxi if the taxi-driver had not slammed on his brakes. The bus had been forced to swerve to avoid the taxi. But the lady was not disposed to be reasonable: her fury had been directed solely and eloquently at Alfred, reducing him to a creature of shrinking misery, whose stammering offers of compensation were brushed contemptuously aside.

Once out on the pavement, Alfred, scarlet-faced and perspiring, looked wildly around to see if any of the alighted passengers might be a colleague. He recognised no-one but, for weeks afterwards, his dread of ridicule made him suspicious of any suppressed word or covert glance, fearing that somehow the story had got about and it was many months before he could bring himself to board another bus in the Strand.

On this bright spring morning Alfred directed his steps to Hobart's Wood. It was not a particularly large wood, but so overgrown and dense that the clamour of the outside world, its restless immediacy, could not penetrate. It was a favourite place of Alfred's. Here, in the stillness and peace, anyone receptive could sense nature as a thing eternal, timeless, unchanging, recognising change only in the repetitive passing of season into season, year following year. Alfred was receptive. In the seclusion of Hobart's Wood he became a different person, relaxed, released, sensitive to an atmosphere sympathetic to his 'sensations', his secret life, as he liked to think of them. Secret they were, being something else which Alfred kept jealously to himself but, infrequent and transitory, they could hardly be termed a life although they were, indeed, flashes of awareness of something – an intangible something – outside his everyday existence. The prosaic Alfred had never been tempted into flights of fancy and they were not that: they were not born out of conscious thought. Coming unbidden and with only brief warning, they left in Alfred, fleetingly, a feeling which was a strange mixture of exhaustion and exhilaration. He accepted these occurrences passively – he could not, in any case, have frustrated them – and with an almost sensuous pleasure. But he had never, until his retirement, attempted deliberately to encourage them. Extra-sensory experience was a subject which had never attracted his interest, and any suggestion that his sensations were not unique, would have disappointed and even distressed him.

He had only once spoken of the matter. He had been a young man, out walking with a distant cousin of his father's, when the feeling had inconsiderately swept over him, leaving him – as was usual – momentarily unsteady. The cousin had asked if he felt unwell and Alfred's innate honesty had obliged him to make a truthful – though not necessarily specific – reply. The cousin had said, 'Blood pressure, my dear fellow – better do something about it.'

What Alfred did about it was avoid any future confidences. There had never been, in any case, anyone close enough or sympathetic enough – not even his sister – in whom he had ever felt a wish, or need, to confide. Although kindly, he was reticent by nature and gave an impression of aloofness which did not encourage friendship. He was well aware that his colleagues and acquaintances regarded him as something resembling an efficient machine, reliable and without emotion. They would have received any hint of his experiences with incredulity turning, possibly, to amusement. Alfred's dread of ridicule was strong but, even stronger, was his fear that discussion, the cold scrutiny of logic, would destroy this precious thing.

It had not always been a precious thing. For some time he had regarded it with distrust and disquiet but, as the years passed and nothing of significance appeared to be associated with it, no physical or mental disorder, he began to regard it as a gift, a privilege; to believe that, for some reason he did not question, he had been singled out to have experiences unfettered by time and space. It had started when he was quite a young boy and had been taken to the cinema by a visiting aunt. The film (he could remember nothing of the story) was set in some primitive, far-off land. Those were the days of the silent screen so there were no sound effects to enhance the atmosphere, no technicolour to bring vividness to the scenery, but the young Alfred began to be conscious of an eerie feeling of involvement: he was not watching the scene from a safe cinema seat, he was actually in that native place; he could feel the oppressive humidity of the jungle, could smell the hot, dank vegetation, hear the sound of trickling water and of birds' wings among the branches overhead and their strange calls and chatter: so dense and towering were the great trees that no light penetrated the gloom beneath them. But, above all, it was familiar; he knew what was out of sight beyond that native hut, how the land, thickly wooded, fell steeply down to open scrub and sun-scorched plain. And there was a pervading sense of menace – undefined – brooding.

He emerged from the cinema silent and shaken. If he had mentioned the experience it would more than probably have been dismissed as due to the over-active imagination of a child. But Alfred was not an imaginative child. To begin with the matter was much on his mind, and the cinema experience was repeated from time to time, but the translocation was only momentary, a sudden flash of awareness quenched immediately, like a brilliant light switching on and off. Over the years the occurrences became less frequent and less definitive, and there was no recurrence of the premonition of danger. They would be presaged by a heightening of the senses, a tingling of the skin, slight breathlessness, a feeling of insubstantiality; and then would come detachment, a sense of infinite space, of being outside the confines of his body and environment. A fleeting moment only, and then normality was again in control.

After his retirement, with time on his hands, Alfred let his mind dwell more on these things and, in Hobart's Wood, he had sensed an affinity with the strange illusory power by which he believed himself to be possessed. It was an ordinary English wood but, possibly because of its great age, in its own way primitive. Some of the massive oaks had counted the seasons for three hundred years; there were beeches, shining freshly green on this spring morning, sycamores dripping their pendant blooms, and the white poplars their flamboyant catkins. Young saplings challenged their elders for living room and, half concealed by ferns and tall bronze grasses, were the trunks of old trees which had lost the fight for survival, lying close by their moss-shrouded stumps: there were thickets of bramble and holly and the occasional spindle-wood. The path under Alfred's feet was a patchwork of moss and stunted grass and the ubiquitous dandelion. Beside the path were primroses in smiling groups with, here and there, an early bluebell. Overhead among the branches, where new-born leaves were gilded by the sunshine, sparrows and finches, blackbirds and thrushes and, on the highest boughs, rooks sang or squabbled. In the distance the solitary cuckoo sent out his haunting call. Unidentified small creatures rustled the undergrowth and, only feet in front of Alfred, a robin, unafraid, searched the path for food. Alfred was conscious of none of these things. There had been a hint that morning of the familiar heightening of his senses and the feeling grew stronger as he entered the wood. Deliberately he kept his mind open and expectant, and suddenly, the illusion was there. But this time it was not transitory, flashing in and out of his consciousness. The shadows beneath the trees became heavier, shutting out the sunshine: the air closed in on him hot, damp, and oppressive, and the sense of menace was there, an almost palpable thing.

Alfred felt neither unease nor surprise: nor was he surprised to find himself, on rounding a bend in the path, face to face with a lion.

---

Simba was very unhappy. He was tired, he was hungry, and he was thirsty. He had walked for many hours and, in all the long night, had found nowhere to rest in this unfamiliar and alien world in which he found himself. He was not a young cat and, while he could still respond to the demands of his circus performance, his muscles were not accepting without protest the strain of prolonged and unaccustomed exercise. His feet were strangers to hard pavements and rutted lanes and his pads were sore and burning. He plodded forward, great head drooping low between massive shoulders as if they could no longer support its weight. Parched tongue lolling out from between dry lips, jowls swaying as he moved, he looked neither to left nor right, his little bloodshot eyes seeing only the path ahead through a haze of weariness. It had been a cold night and Simba was not used to cold nights. His quarters at the circus were warm, and there was plenty to eat and drink. Leaving that haven had not been a good idea: he was too old for adventures. He would have returned thankfully, but he did not know the way.

Like so many momentous events in life the adventure had had its beginning in a triviality – an irritation in his shoulder. To relieve it he had rubbed against the door of his cage and the door had slid partly open. The bolt had been insecure for some time, but no-one had thought much about it: Simba was placid and lazy, and attention to safety where he was concerned had become cursory. But Simba was a cat, and it is in the nature of all cats, small and large, domestic or wild, to be curious. Startled and distrustful he had at first retreated to the back of his cage but then, moving slowly round by the bars until he reached the outside, with freedom an unfamiliar excitement heating his blood, he had loped across the field where the Company was encamped and beyond into the twilit countryside. He was not missed for several hours by which time no nearby traces of him could be found.

His disappearance was reported on radio news that morning – the news, which Alfred had not been able to hear. The announcement said that the lion was not thought to be dangerous: he liked people: he had been hand-reared when his mother rejected him and had been bought by Cookman's Circus while still a cub: there he was on friendly terms with everyone. But it would not be prudent, the newsreader warned, to approach him; any sightings should be reported to the police.

It was not true that Simba liked people. There was a bond of affection between him and his trainer, Greg Packett – Sinbad of the bill-boards – but towards the rest of the circus personnel he was indifferent. And of people in general, outside that little domestic group, he had no knowledge. The nightly audiences beyond the glaring lights over the circus ring were not distinguishable as people; they were a blur, from which came clapping, shouting and cheering, a confusion of noise. To him the blur and the noise combined as one thing and were part of the routine of his life. What it signified he neither knew nor cared.

Now he was approaching a wood through an area of shrubs and a scattering of trees, not unlike the African bush. In these surroundings there was familiarity. Although born in a north European zoo of parents also born in captivity, Simba was, nevertheless, a creature of the wild and the bush was his natural habitat. But then be became conscious of change: the trees grew closer and taller, throwing black shadows across the sunlit path: the underbrush was denser and dank, the air humid and oppressive. In the heavy gloom, he was uneasy. It was then that Alfred appeared on the path in front of him.

Man and beast both stood still, recognition immediate and mutual. This was not their first meeting: there was unfinished business between them.

Simba drew back a pace, little eyes narrowed, glinting, malevolent. Yellow lips curling back from yellow fangs, he snarled softly. Slowly his hindquarters lowered, quivering, his tasselled tail sweeping the path, the muscles taut in his powerful shoulders tensed for the spring. Alfred also took a step backward, without conscious thought unhooking his umbrella from his left arm and tossing it into his right hand. It fell into his grasp at the exact point of balance. As the lion, with a deafening roar, launched himself into the air, Alfred turned his body, flung back his arm, and then lunged forward, driving the umbrella spear into the body of the huge cat as it fell on him. It pierced Simba's heart and splintered as the great weight, with Alfred crushed beneath, struck the ground. Alfred's neck snapped against the stump of a fallen tree.

Simba's terrifying roar, ripping through the quiet of this peaceful world, sent all the birds clattering wildly out of the trees with panic cries – the rooks raucously protesting their outrage. They wheeled above the wood, anxious and fretful; only the cuckoo, intent on courtship, seemed unaffected by the commotion, continuing to pipe out his two-toned call.

Gradually the birds returned, still ruffled, still complaining. But nothing now disturbed the normality of the April morning. A speckled spider, oblivious to the drama, explored the bark of the fallen tree where Alfred lay. A vole, peeping out from under autumn's bounty of fallen leaves, wrinkled her nose at the unfamiliar smell of the lion's body nearby and then, losing interest, withdrew to continue foraging for food. A squirrel, emerging from his drey and seeing nothing to alarm him, flashed along the branch of a tree. It was as if the moment of violence and uproar had never been. Only the motionless bodies on the sun-dappled path bore witness.

Caught on a low twig of a nearby tree, as though tidily placed on a coat peg, hung Alfred's bowler hat.

# *The Apple Loft*

Jane heard the shriek of the train whistle and braced herself for the inevitable. The coast express rounded the bend half a mile up the line and, in a few moments, thundered past the side of the house, a bare fifty yards away. From somewhere near the top of the house there came a resounding bang and, although she had braced herself for it, Jane jumped.

'Frank, when are you going to fix that door?'

Her husband looked up briefly from his morning paper. 'Remind me on Sunday,' he said and returned to his page-three girls.

'I reminded you last Sunday,' said Jane, 'and the Sunday before, and the one before that, and …'

'Here, hold on.' Frank emerged again from behind his paper. 'It hasn't been doing it that long.'

'It seems to have been doing it for ever,' said Jane.

'And what about all those other Sunday jobs lined up for me?' said Frank, 'Like painting the bathroom, mending the fence, picking the apples and putting them up there.'

'So what's wrong with Saturdays?'

'I play golf,' said Frank firmly, 'besides, it needs a new catch and I haven't got one.'

'Then get one,' said Jane, 'it'll need new hinges as well if you don't do something about it soon.'

'Dear lady, the shop hasn't opened when I go in the morning and it's shut by the time I finish in the evening.'

'Excuses, excuses,' said Jane, exasperated.

'You're nagging again, woman.' Frank got up from the breakfast table and gave his wife an affectionate peck on the cheek. 'I'll see to it, though I don't really understand all the fuss. Leave the thing open if it bothers you so much, it can't bang then.'

Jane accompanied him to the door. 'Perhaps I'll get someone in the village to do it,' was her parting shot as he got into his car and drove through the gates. It was an empty threat: the village boasted only one small general store-cum-post office and no jobbing workmen that she knew of.

'Men!' she grumbled as she climbed the two flights of stairs to the loft, 'and he's taken the paper with him.' The door, which was an upright one in the wall under the sloping roof, was hinged at the bottom, forming a ramp which gave easy access into the loft under the eaves. It was lying open now across the landing. 'I'm not going to leave it open,' thought Jane mutinously, 'it's supposed to be shut,' and she slammed the door with such vehemence that the shaky catch almost gave way again and there came an uneasy creaking from the other side.

The express went past four times a day, twice in each direction, and the house, indifferent to all the other trains, responded to it; it vibrated. Whether it was a thrill of pleasure or a shiver of fear Jane hadn't decided but, either way, there was this slight vibration which had been enough, over the past several weeks, to dislodge the ageing catch on the loft door. Jane loved the shadowy loft, the dim shapes of the apples lying on their cardboard trays on the rickety wooden staging, and their sweet smell.

She loved everything about the old one-time farmhouse; had done from the moment she saw it, three years ago, when she and Frank had been looking for somewhere away from the town where he worked, and its ever-increasing noise and pollution. The double-fronted house was wide and low, apart from the centre gable where the loft was situated: it was deep thatched and the oak-beamed rooms were spacious. It stood in an acre of ground, a garden circling the front and sides and with an orchard at the back. The narrow road in front ran over the level crossing and joined up with the main road to town, twelve miles away: easy commuting distance. The village lay five minutes walk in the other direction and provided a two-hourly bus service into town.

There were only a few scattered cottages in the vicinity but Jane did not mind the isolation; rather she welcomed it. Here was the peace she had longed for during years of town dwelling, and there was plenty to keep her busy. She had made the garden into quite a show-piece, with its lawns and flower beds, its rose arches and ornamental pool. She liked to fancy that passengers on the trains saw it as an oasis in the desert of featureless fields, drab sidings and dusty hedges along the line and were refreshed by it. The only fly in her ointment was the loft door, and she had to admit to herself that she had let it become something of an obsession. She contemplated going to buy a catch herself, 'but he'd be sure to find some fault with it,' she thought uncharitably.

But by the time she sat down to a late morning coffee her normal sunny nature had reasserted itself. The express would be along again shortly but she was determined to ignore it. The sudden knock on the front door surprised her; casual visitors were rare. She opened the door to an unsavoury-looking character, unshaven, unwashed, with lank greasy hair. His leering smile revealed gaps in discoloured teeth. Jane's impulse was to slam the door, but innate courtesy made her wait for him to state his business.

'Any odd jobs for me, lady?' It was an unpleasant, ingratiating voice, 'I c'd do wiv a copper or two.'

'I'm sorry, I haven't.'

'I c'n mend fences, do a bit o' diggin', or slap on a bit o' paint if you gotta shed what wants it.'

'I haven't, thank you. Good day.' But it was too late, his foot was in the door. She backed as he pushed his way in. 'Wh – what are you doing? How dare you. Get out at once or I'll call my husband.' Anger and alarm made her voice unnaturally shrill.

He sneered, 'But 'e ain't 'ere is 'e? I see 'im go orf in 'is motor.'

'He ... he came back,' stammered Jane, 'he's upstairs. And I'll call my dog.'

The man laughed, an ugly laugh, 'Then where's 'is wheels? You can't fool me, lady.' He had pushed her against the wall, pinning her there with a hand on either side of her. His breath on her face was foul. Jane felt panic clutching her throat.

'Look, she gasped, 'my purse is on the kitchen table. Take what you want and go. Please.'

'Oh, I'm gonna take what I want all right,' the man said, and his voice had become menacing. 'Now why don't you be nice and kind to me – make it easy on yourself.'

As the horror of his meaning sank in Jane screamed and began to struggle wildly as he started dragging her towards the living room, his fingers digging painfully into her shoulders. He swore, letting out a stream of filthy language. Jane screamed again, 'Frank! Marty!'

Marty didn't come. Marty was probably chasing imaginary rabbits in the back field. He would, in any case, have greeted the intruder like a long-lost brother. All the world was Marty's friend, which made him endearing and utterly useless.

Frank didn't come either, of course: but the express did. In her terror Jane had not heard it, but the loft door reacted true to form; it crashed open. The man's grip on her shoulders slackened as he shot a startled and incredulous look up the stairs. Jane seized her opportunity and wrenched herself free. 'Frank!' she screamed again. There came a new sound from above, the sound of thumping and bumping on the stairs, like running footsteps. The man turned and fled. Jane slammed the door and leaned against it trembling, watching the apples pile up at the foot of the stairs. The crashing door had been doing the ancient staging no favours, nor had the violence of her morning protest, and a section of it had finally been jolted away from its supports, allowing its loaded trays to slide off and tip the apples out, over the ramp and down the stairs.

## *The Corner Table*

She had prepared herself for the inevitability of change, not its absence. But the little café in the small-town high street looked exactly as she remembered it, even to the peeling green paint on the window frames and door. There must, surely, have been many coats of paint over the years since she and Rob had idly picked off the brittle flakes as they loitered outside chatting, fooling, before going in for a milkshake or lemonade. For a fleeting moment nostalgia caught her breath and she was a teenager again.

The door stood open. To her recollection the door had always been open, except in the worst of bad weather. It opened back on the table in the window corner, isolating it from the rest of the room. That had been their favourite table, her's and Rob's.

She crossed the road and went in, half eager, half shy, a nervous fluttering in the pit of her stomach. In her imagination she had pictured this meeting many times as the date for it drew near. Rob would be waiting: he would come forward with hands outstretched, smiling that huge smile that seemed to crease up the whole of his face. She had never entertained the slightest doubt that recognition would be immediate and mutual. The years had not neglected them, of course, as they appeared to have neglected the café, but there would be chemistry, an awareness. They would sit at the corner table and talk. They had always been able to talk – nonstop. And there would be so much to talk about.

But no-one came forward to greet her. After the sunshine outside, the interior of the café was dim but she could see that it was empty, apart from one couple who were sitting at the corner table. Disappointment was almost physical. It was like meeting a chill wind and, with the abrupt collapse of built-up expectation, she was momentarily at a loss. She had never doubted that he would be there. But then she was early, very early: it still wanted forty minutes to the meeting time. Rob would not expect her to be so early: punctuality had never been one of her virtues. Any minute now he would be there, and a little time to settle down and compose herself might not be a bad thing. She took her coffee to a table from which she could watch the door and the street outside. She pictured his tall figure coming through the door, upright, brisk of step, and having about him a presence, a distinction, as befitted a man who had risen to the top of his profession. Then she would move forward to greet him. He wouldn't be expecting that. The thought of his surprise brought a smile to her lips. Her eyes now accustomed to the soft light inside the café, she gazed around and was again gripped by a sense of the past. The room was caught in a time warp. As with the outside, incredibly, almost nothing had changed and the past was no further away than yesterday. The same scuffed brown lino (though protected now by strips of heavy, ridged plastic), its pattern discernable only in the odd places away from the lines of passage. They were the same glass-topped tables with the black and white tile pattern under the glass. By craning her neck she thought she could see the thin line of light caught along the crack: so even the the tables had kept their accustomed places. One thing was missing – the juke box. She had forgotten juke boxes until now: it was years since she had seen one. What happened to them? She had enjoyed the juke box. You put your sixpence in (when you had one to spare) and pressed the button for the tune you wanted. Her favourite had been Bing Crosby crooning 'Love in Bloom'. Rob had preferred the more lively 'Sing as we Go', sung by Gracie Fields. When they had only one sixpence between them they argued. It was always Rob who gave way. The old tunes started running through her brain: there was melody in songs in those days.

She kept glancing towards the couple at the corner table, hoping for some indication that they were about to move, but they seemed in no hurry. They had looked up briefly as she entered and then returned to the contemplation of their empty cups. The man, elderly, with wispy grey hair, sat hunched round-shouldered over the table: the woman – possibly his daughter – played with her spoon. They did not converse.

If only they would go so that they could move across. It was the second disappointment, finding that table occupied. She had looked forward to sitting there with Rob. That table had been important to them, their private retreat, and it seemed the fitting place for their reunion. It had been witness to all their youthful plans and secrets, and it was the table where Rob had asked her to marry him. The proposal had come out of the blue, taking her aback. He had suddenly reached for her hand and said – blurting out the words as if in a great hurry – 'Marry me, Meg. I love you very much. Couldn't we get married – soon – please?' His hand trembled a little and his face flushed. She had stammered, giggled, self-conscious and embarrassed. She was a very immature eighteen-year-old, only just emerging from the comfortable world of childhood. Rob, a year older, was the boy from over the back she had played with all her life: there had never been any hint of romance. Now, suddenly, it was almost as if the young soldier in his smart new uniform was a stranger.

'Oh Rob, I don't know ... I hadn't though ...' Her face, too, had flushed up. 'I like you a lot, really I do. But we've always just been friends. I hadn't thought that way. I'm sorry Rob, I'm not ready...' Her voice faltered and stopped. She was caught in a conflict of emotions: there was surprise and shock together with resentment at this abrupt destruction of their easy, undemanding relationship, at the discomfiture he was causing her; and there was also distress at hurting him.

'But love grows out of friendship' said Rob, 'it's a good basis for marriage. I've loved you for a long time. I know I could make you happy. Sorry to spring it on you like this.' He attempted a grin. 'I would have waited and wooed you properly – bended knee and all that – if it hadn't been for this wretched war. Now there's no time to wait, we don't know if there is going to be a future for us. Couldn't we get married and take all the happiness we can, while we can?' It was the attitude of many young people in those days.

She had shifted uncomfortably in her chair, for the first time in her life uncomfortable in his company. 'Oh Rob, I'm sorry. It's too big a thing when I'm not sure. I don't want to settle down yet, I'm just not ready. Let's leave it a bit.' She had stared at the crack in the table top, reluctant to meet his eyes. After an awkward silence he released her hand with a sigh. 'Well, think about it,' he said, 'and keep thinking about it, because I shall keep on asking. That's a promise.'

'Or a threat,' she teased, trying to establish their normal mood of light-hearted comradeship. 'Anyway, if we don't meet again until after the war, and the war lasts for years and years, we will probably have forgotten one another.'

'Don't be daft.' His voice was uncharacteristically sharp.

'All sorts of things could have happened.' She was being deliberately perverse, unwilling to accept any kind of commitment.

'All sorts of what things?' He was scornful. 'But OK, then we'll vow it: that will make sure of it. Vowing is binding.'

'Oh, Rob, that's silly,' she protested. 'What are we vowing, anyway?'

'To meet again, of course, no matter what happens.' Rob fished in a pocket for his diary and tore out a blank page. 'Vowing it' was something they had invented as children and was childishly simple, a variation of 'cross my heart and hope to die'. They took it very seriously and had never broken a vow. But they were little childish matters, nothing with far-reaching implications such as this.

She watched a little unhappily as Rob wrote their names on the paper. The three letters of both their names, printed one above the other formed a little square.

'How long shall we make it?' he asked; 'something impossibly extreme; let's say fifty years.'

'Fifty years!' her voice rose in a squeak. 'We'll be old fogies by then, no hair, no teef.' There spoke the arrogance of youth, she now thought, which considered anyone over the age of forty as approaching dotage.

Ignoring her Rob kissed the paper saying 'I vow it' and passed it to her to do the same. Then he drew a circle round the two names, an unbroken ring meaning that the vow could not be broken and, folding the paper, slipped it back inside his diary.

'Don't look so glum. As soon as we meet again after the war it's cancelled. This is just to provide against the unthinkable. Eleven o'clock on the eighth of August fifty years from now. Make a note of it.'

She had made a note of it and here she was. It was the date and the place and approaching the hour, but there was no Rob. She felt the first faint qualm of unease. She had never doubted that he would come. The whole idea had, after all, been his. But she chided herself for being impatient. He might have a long journey and rail and road traffic were always subject to delays. If he came in the next twenty minutes he would still be on time.

That had been their last meeting. Rob went away to do his military training and then was drafted overseas. She joined the Land Army and met Doyle. And suddenly life became a magical existence in which perception was enhanced; nothing was ordinary any more. To walk was to dance, to dance was to float on air, to talk was to sing. There was music in silence, shining lights in the blackout: there were bells and butterflies and breathlessness. In short all the heady exhilaration missing from her relationship with Rob and, in under six weeks, she was a G.I. bride.

Rob had acknowledged the news of her marriage with a brief note wishing her well and that had been their last direct contact. There had, however, been a two-way passage of family news through their sisters: her elder sister and Rob's had been close friends. So she knew that he had taken a degree course after the war, qualifying as a civil engineer, and at the time of his retirement was deputy head of a well-established local firm. And he would know that she had been widowed three years back. This exchange of information had ended abruptly, however, when both sisters tragically fell victim to a killer 'flu' virus two winters ago. Up to that time Rob had not married. She wondered if it was because he had looked upon her as his only love. She hoped not: she did not want to feel responsible for him having led a lonely and barren life. But it was a flattering thought.

Doyle had been good to her; America had been good to her; and time, also had treated her kindly. Fifty years on from the vowing she was far from being an old fogey. Expensive bridgework had taken care of her teeth and the contours of her face; her unruly auburn curls, now silvered, were disciplined and stylishly coiffured. Her skin was only faintly lined, her make-up skilful and discreet. She had worn too much make-up in those days; most girls did and the boys seemed to like it. She had a tolerant affection for the leggy (in her mother's unflattering terms, scraggy) eighteen-year-old she had been but she bore little resemblance to her. In its natural progress to maturity her figure had become what she liked to describe as 'rounded', and it was well served by the elegance of her outfit. She knew herself to be a well-preserved and handsome woman, and was anticipating with pleasure Rob's appreciative admiration. He, too, would have matured, of course, with success and responsibility, growing in assurance and stature. But, underneath, he would still be the same dear Rob and, to him, she would still be the old Meg. She had been Margaret from the day she met Doyle because he said it was his favourite name, but she had a fondness for the old pet name and it would be pleasant to hear it again.

The hands of her watch were nudging eleven o'clock. This was so unlike Rob. Well, it was unlike Rob used to be. People did change: circumstances and experience changed them. Rob had remained with her over the years as a fond memory and she had thought of him frequently in the years since her widowhood. She wondered if they would have married after the war if she had not met Doyle or if, during those years of separation, they would have grown apart. How much further apart might fifty years not have placed them? Perhaps the expectation she had cherished of meeting the Rob of fifty years ago was stupidly unrealistic. They might meet as strangers. Had she come all this way just to lay a ghost? Growing anxiety sent her mind stumbling through these thoughts and doubts but she shrugged them away; it was unthinkable that he would have changed: he would just be an older version of the same Rob. He would be sure to arrive soon, remorsefully apologetic, with a logical explanation for his lateness.

The popularity of the café seemed to have waned since the old days, when it was full of activity, of noise, of laughter. Today it came to life only twice; once when three boisterous children came in to buy cartons of orange juice, and once when a little elderly woman came in for a coffee. She was carrying a little elderly dog of uncertain ancestry which forgot its toilet training as soon as it was placed on the floor. They both made a hurried and surreptitious departure. The incident could barely induce a smile. There were no other customers, and no-one remotely approximating to her mental image of Rob even passed outside.

Ten past eleven ... twenty past. Her fingers drumming on the table betrayed anxiety and impatience, the build-up of nervous tension. As the minutes dragged the monotony fed her growing despondency. It was twenty-five to twelve. She began to feel that her aloneness was conspicuous: it was like being abandoned. Her only company was the silent couple at the corner table , and they were unwelcome. Why did they not go? Reason pointed out that they had as much right to stay as she had, but she was in no mood to listen to reason. She was becoming obsessed by the wholly illogical belief that, if she could sit at that table, Rob would come.

At twelve o'clock she at last acknowledged the fear that had been nagging her for the past hour. He was not coming. There was no point in pretending any longer. There was no point in waiting any longer. He was not coming. What a fool she had been. Of course Rob would not have expected her to come: he would have given her credit for more sense. No woman in her right mind would travel half way across the world for the sake of a game. Because that was all it was, a silly childish game.

She felt small, as if she had shrunk in the time she had been sitting in the café. Tears of mortification and disillusion threatened to disgrace her: she quelled them with fierce, self-protective anger – at herself – at him. He had let her down. He had stayed away when he could at least have come on the off-chance that she would be there, however sure he may have felt that she would not. If he had to travel the length of England that was nothing compared with the distance that she had come.

She gathered up her gloves and handbag with quick, jerky movements and walked out of the shop. As she passed the couple by the door she looked at them with hostility, a quite irrational resentment. They watched her with indifference. Grey people, she thought spitefully, grey faces, grey lives. Once outside she made her way back towards the station, tears of hurt and betrayal blurring the sun-bright street. She walked hurriedly, as if trying to distance herself as quickly as possible from the scene of her humiliation. She was cold, a deep cold that the August heat could not reach. But as she walked her anger died, leaving only an aching sadness. Rob would not have let her down deliberately. He had forgotten, that was all. After all, fifty years was a very long time.

A little later, back in the café, the woman at the corner table said gently, 'I think we should go now, Matron will be getting worried.' He nodded, obedient as a child and, rising stiffly to his feet, followed her out into the street. He moved clumsily, leaning heavily on his stick and dragging one foot. He was recovering well from his stroke earlier in the year but walking still presented some difficulty. He walked slowly, his eyes bleak with disappointment. When you pin your hopes on a dream, they die when the dream fades on waking. It was a lot to expect of someone living half the world away, and yet he had been quite certain she would come. But she would not have stayed away deliberately, of that he was sure. She had forgotten, that was all. After all, fifty years was a very long time.

# *The Dog and Duck*

'Blast!' I said, and followed that up with several more choice expletives. I pulled the starter and the engine struggled back to life. I trod on the accelerator, though without much hope; the wheels churned the soft snow and settled the car deeper into the drift. The engine sulked into silence.

It had been madness, of course, to attempt driving across the moor in the light of the ominous weather forecast; there had already been heavy falls of snow. Good sense had certainly advised against it. But I had been deaf to good sense. It was Christmas Eve and I was invited to spend Christmas with friends. With two-thirds of the journey completed I wasn't going to give it up easily. And what was forty miles? Nothing in normal circumstances, but these were not normal circumstances. The rutted, ice-packed road had little sympathy with my foolhardiness, and even less respect for the car. Progress had been tediously slow and uncomfortable and, before half an hour had passed, the weather-gods had flung at me the full force of their spite. It didn't just snow, it came down as if some huge tip-up lorry in the heavens was shedding its load, a load without limit. It didn't just blow, the wind howled and shrieked and buffeted the car from side to side. In the drift we were at least sheltered from the wind, but I'd swear that its shrieks were now of demonic laughter: it had won, it had shown this insolent bighead who was boss.

So here I was, wherever 'here' was. I had no idea if I was still on – or to be accurate, had just skidded off – the right road. It was now dark. I appeared to have two options, neither particularly attractive; to brave the elements in the hope of finding habitation, or to spend the night in the car. To hope for succour from a passing driver was futile; no other fool would be out on a night like this. I started to open the car door. There was already resistance from the deep snow and I closed it again quickly, shrinking from the icy blast which greeted me. The car, at least, was warm for the moment; the heater had died with the engine but the warmth would last for a few hours. In that white hell outside I could take a couple of steps away from the car and never find it again. A man could die out there. So there was really one option; to stay where I was.

Then, as I stared moodily through the windscreen, against which the snow was rapidly piling up, I glimpsed what I thought was a spot of light in the distance. It disappeared in the snow flurries, then reappeared. Could there be another benighted traveller ahead? If that was the rear light of a car it, like mine, wasn't going anywhere. It never moved. I rubbed the mist from the inside of the glass with my sleeve and stared intently. There was a sudden upward eddy in the swirling snow which momentarily cleared the distance and, with incredulous delight, I made out another spot of light, and another. I could hardy believe my luck; they were windows. I had come to grief near one of the few isolated inns along that road. I struggled with the car door and forced it open far enough to squeeze through. Immediately I sank into snow up to my knees and floundered with the utmost difficulty up to the road. There I was at the mercy of the wind. It tore at me viciously, whipping stinging snow into my face and eyes, stopping my breath and throwing me off balance. Gasping and staggering I fought towards those beckoning lights; they grew slowly larger and brighter, encouraging with their promise of warmth and shelter.

At length I stumbled, panting, under the porch of the inn and hammered at the door. It was flung open almost at once by a big, jovial man who grabbed my arm and practically snatched me over the threshold, slamming the door behind me in the face of the blizzard which tried to follow. Baulked of its prey the wind shrieked and shook the door savagely.

'My dear sir, my dear sir,' the man's hands flapped over my head and shoulders, brushing off the snow, 'what a night to be stranded. Yes,' in reply to my half articulated query, 'of course we can give you a room.' He seized my hand with his large fleshy one and pumped it up and down. 'Bonser's the name, Eric Bonser. Delighted to make your acquaintance. Get that wet coat off and I'll fetch something to warm you up.' He whisked away, moving surprisingly lightly for such a big man, and was back before I was out of my coat with a large brandy, which he pressed into my hand. 'It's on the house. Go and thaw out by the fire. We'll be sitting to table in about half an hour. You couldn't have timed it better,' he chuckled. 'It's turkey tonight; goose tomorrow. Susie! Another setting for this young gentleman.' The buxom country lass who bustled forward could only have been his daughter: the same round, rosy cheeks and laughing eyes, the same shining brown curls. The white apron on her red dress was crisp and spotless.

'I'll get a fire going in your room,' she said, as she set a place for me at table, which was overflowing with festive fare. 'I hope you won't mind the second floor.' I assured her I would love the second floor – I would have been grateful for the floor under the staircase on such a night – and asked if there was a 'phone I might use to let my friends know where I was.

'You're welcome to try,' she said, 'it's on the end of the bar, but it was dead when I wanted it a while back.'

I tried, but it gave no hint of having accomplished the miracle of resurrection. 'Expect the line's down somewhere along,' said Susie cheerfully, 'it's not unusual in this sort of weather.'

I took my brandy and joined a number of other guests who were grouped around the huge fireplace at the far end of the room. The fireplace housed a huge blazing fire which was piled high with tarred wooden road blocks (I concluded that the road outside had recently been resurfaced). Helped by the wind in the chimney the fire roared and spat fiercely, sending out generous warmth and a myriad of sparks. A smiling grey-haired couple made room for me beside them on a settee, introducing themselves as Charles and Ada.

'How was your journey?' asked Charles. 'We were lucky, we got here yesterday before all this started.' I explained that, for me, this was an unscheduled visit.

'I was crazy to start out with a blizzard threatening,' I said, 'I didn't deserve this good luck – breaking down so close to hospitality

– a car marooned in a snowdrift is not the most festive of places to spend Christmas Eve.'

'Oh, it's festive enough here,' laughed Ada, 'Mr Bonser – we call him Bonzo because he's just like a big, floppy, friendly puppy – is a grand host and great fun. He has this house party every year and we wouldn't miss it, would we Charles?'

Her husband grunted. 'Treats us all like a lot of kids,' he grinned, 'and we're all daft enough to enjoy it.'

There were, perhaps, half a dozen couples in the big room, all middle-aged to elderly, all chatting and relaxed in an atmosphere of cheerfulness and bonhomie. The room itself was brilliant with lights and gay with paper chains, gold balls and holly. In one corner a magnificent Christmas tree, sparkling with fairy lights and tinsel, reached its branches almost to the ceiling.

While we dined, unobtrusive seasonal music provided a background accompaniment to the clatter of knives and forks, and tongues loosened by good food and good humour: jokes and laughter flowed with the wine. With the coffee came a gift for everyone off the tree. Mine was a leather key-ring embossed, in gold leaf, with the inn sign: a pleasing memento, I thought. After dinner we played the kind of games I remembered from childhood parties – musical chairs, hunt the thimble, kiss in the ring, postman's knock, pinning the tail on the donkey. We danced; we sang carols and old music-hall choruses until even alcoholic lubrication, which was plentiful, lost the power to soothe the croak out of our voices. We were foolishly and gloriously happy, and it was well into the early hours before the party broke up.

My room was cheerfully warm with a blazing fire in the grate. Like the one downstairs it had been fed with the tarred wooden blocks, and was spitting and crackling fiercely, sending sparks high up the chimney. I eyed it a little apprehensively, but I had partaken freely of the wine of the house and was no sooner between the sheets than I was asleep. It was, however, a troubled sleep. I seemed to be aware of a great deal of noise and commotion and, in spite of the warm room and soft bed, I was cold. But I did not wake until I felt someone shaking my shoulder and heard a voice saying, 'Are you all right, sir?' I opened my eyes to the thin light of early morning and looked up into the concerned eyes of two policemen. I stared round in bewilderment, trying to gather my wits. I was back in my car, cramped and cold.

'How ... How did I get here?' I gasped.

'Looks like you ran off the road in last night's storm,' said the older of the two, 'Don't you remember? You're lucky we found you. Might not have done if we hadn't been on the look-out. Friends who were expecting you last night got worried when you didn't turn up and called us. You're pretty well covered; we had to clear a space to get the door open.'

'No – I mean I spent the night at the inn, just along the road there. How did I get back here?'

'No inn anywhere near here.' He smiled. 'You've been dreaming. Come, let's get you out and back to the station. You must be frozen.' My mind refused to take this in. As they helped me out of the car and up the slope to the road, my numbed legs stumbling and slithering under me, I was protesting: 'There was a house party, a crowd of us, and the dinner was marvellous, and we played silly games ...' My voice trailed off as I realised I was babbling.

'Wish I had dreams like that,' said the young constable, 'mine are more like nightmares.'

'That's your guilty conscience,' chaffed the other. Then to me, soothingly as to a child, 'You'll feel better with a hot meal inside you.'

The storm had blown itself out; there was even a hint of pink sunrise in the pearl-white sky. I stared down the road in the direction I had taken the evening before. It stretched white, ice-packed, as far as the eye could see, the moor on either side featureless under its hummocks of snow. I turned and looked in the opposite direction: the landscape was the same. There was no sign of habitation.

'There was an inn,' I insisted stubbornly, stupidly.

'Not here, there wasn't.' He guided me towards the Range Rover which was parked a few yards away. 'Never has been.'

'Well, actually there was one once, Sarge,' struck in the younger constable, 'years ago, before my time. And you being new to these parts probably wouldn't know. But I remember my dad speaking of it. Burned down one Christmas morning, it did. Caught 'em all in their beds: there was none got out. Nasty business it was, very nasty.' The chill that ran down my spine had nothing to do with the weather. All those lovely people.

'They shouldn't have burned those tarred blocks,' I muttered. They shot me a puzzled glance, but the constable went on talking.

'*The Dog and Duck*, it was called, and I remember my dad saying the innkeeper had an appropriate nickname – funny how little things stick in your mind – '

'Bonzo,' I said. He swung to face me, 'You know about it?' 'I told you,' I said irritably, 'I was there last night.'

'Er ... yes, well ...' The sergeant's voice was a little uncertain, 'that must have been some dream.' He handed me into the back of the car, tucking a rug solicitously round my knees. As the car was turned carefully to go back the way it had come, I thrust my shaking hands into my pockets for warmth. In one I felt something unfamiliar and drew it out. On my palm lay a leather key-ring embossed with an inn sign: *The Dog and Duck.*

# Ceremony

It should have been memorable, that summer's day in 1970. Indeed it was, though not altogether in the way I would have wished.

Have you ever wondered what the loos are like at Buckingham Palace? I can tell you they are genuine Victorian – those available to the public at any rate. We had one similar in the house where I was born, and which was built at the turn of the century, only ours was smaller. The pan is completely boxed in, the wooden seat fitting flush with the two side walls. Possibly Victorian garments were grateful for that kind of support. The cloakroom was the first place I looked for. Nerves have an embarrassing effect on my inside. But it seemed I was not alone: nearly every woman in the group appeared to have the same priority.

There were perhaps a dozen to twenty of us, and the others, I noted, were all dressed in neat, dark clothes. My misgivings about my own outfit grew. Certainly my dress was basically black, but it had a green and orange pattern I can only describe as jazzy. It was the best I could produce from my wardrobe and I had been under too much pressure at work to take time off to go dress hunting. I'd had to buy a hat. Hat and gloves were essential and I seldom wore either. The hat, bought in desperation from an abysmal selection, did nothing for me and the gloves, also from my wardrobe, were too small. ('Don't give the Queen one of your grips,' my sister had said). When it came to shoes, black sandals were not 'in' I discovered, so I dyed a blue pair. The dye had a pungent smell, which persisted in spite of long exposure to fresh air. I could only hope that other people were not so conscious of it as I was.

From the waiting area we were ushered into a sombre room, dark oak-panelled and hung with dim portraits. There we had to file past a functionary who pinned a small hook below our left shoulders. To me he remarked, 'I hope Her Majesty will be able to see it,' which I took to be a mild reproof at my choice of apparel, and which did little to boost my morale. What with an unsuitable dress, an unbecoming hat, uncomfortable gloves and odorous shoes, I was not feeling my confident best.

We were then drilled on procedure. There were no men in our party and I presumed they were being schooled elsewhere. The instructions were simple but repeated twice to ensure that even the dullest among us could make no mistakes. We would wait in an ante-room which gave into the large room where the ceremony was taking place. When our name was announced we would pass through the door, take five steps forward, turn to the left, another two steps, curtsy, two more steps, and we would be face to face with Her Majesty. She would perform her gracious duty, shake hands, and we would then retire, take four steps backwards, another curtsy, right turn and pass into the ante-room on the other side. So we all lined up, in the wings, as it were, waiting for our cue.

'Don't give the Queen one of your grips.' My sister's voice was in my ears as I heard my name called. Five steps forwards, a smart left turn, two more steps, curtsy with a nice straight back, two more steps and there I was, wearing a fatuous smirk over which I seemed to have no control. 'It' was passed to the Queen on what looked like a cushion, though it probably enjoyed a more grandiose appellation: she had no difficulty in finding the hook.

'What is your work, Miss Balls?' Had she really spoken? It was a mere thread of sound, but I had been prepared for this and stammered out a few well-rehearsed but inadequate words. She nodded gravely, although they could have conveyed little to her. To have explained my work with any degree of lucidity would have taken far more time than I was expected to occupy. She didn't want to know, anyway. Why should she? The question was merely routine, part of the job. And what a deadly boring job it was, among so many others, standing there for hours on end throughout those certain days of the year, being confronted by a succession of faces, most of which she had never seen before and would never see again.

It was over and I could escape. Four steps back, my face still stiff with its fixed grin, and the farewell curtsy. The Queen was fumbling with the brooch on her left shoulder. I found this somewhat disconcerting and a little hurtful that her interest in me, however assumed, could not have been maintained until I left. She did, however, give me a faint smile as I turned and made my exit.

In the small room, which was the first stage on my escape route, I was relieved of the hook and its appendage, the latter being placed in a satin-lined case and handed to me. 'Don't give the Queen one of your grips' was still going through my head like a refrain. And then realisation hit me, and it was a demoralising blow. Because I hadn't, of course. No wonder the poor woman had needed to find something to do with the extended hand I had ignored.

I wonder if I qualify for the Guiness Book of Records, as the only recipient of an MBE who forgot to shake hands.

*The photographs that follow were taken by Joan herself, and have been selected by the publishers to illustrate the author's extraordinary understanding of the beauty of both words and pictures...*

*Joan (left) with her sister Evelyn on the day of her MBE investiture,
Tuesday 28th July 1970*

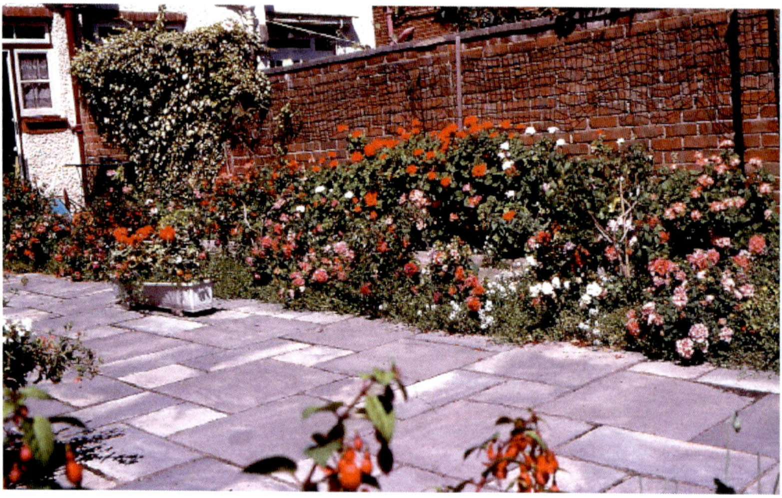

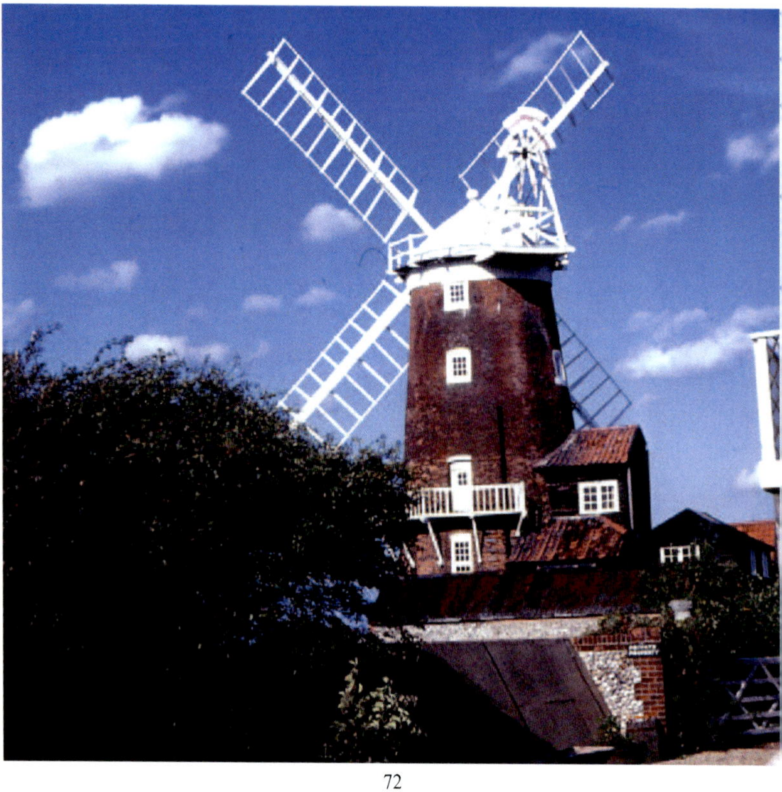

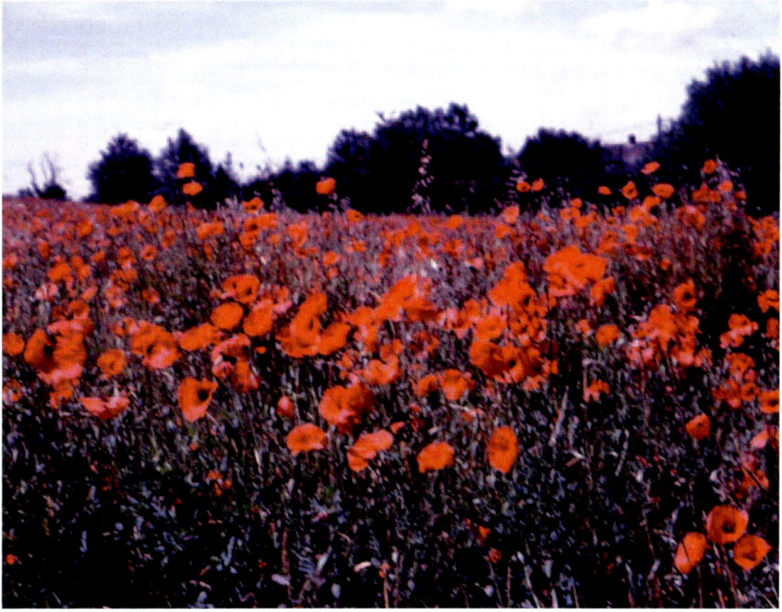

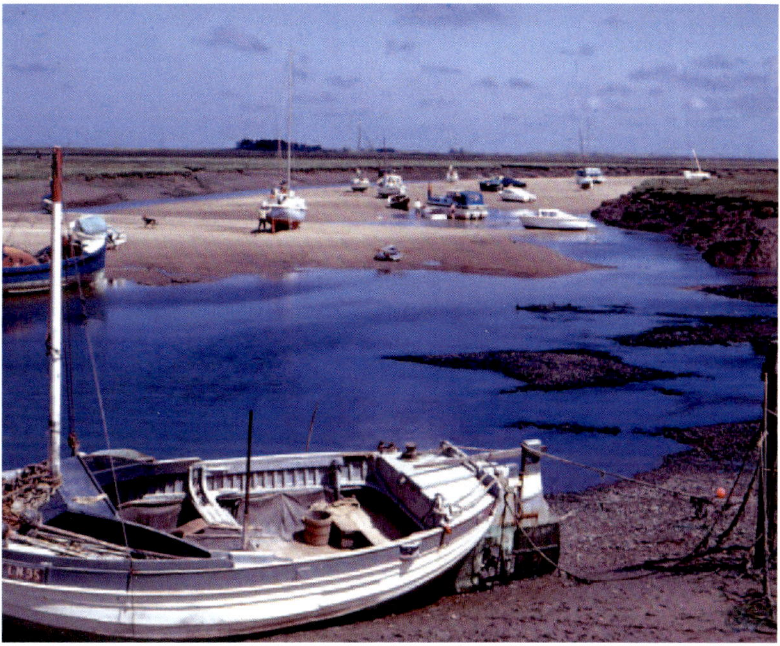

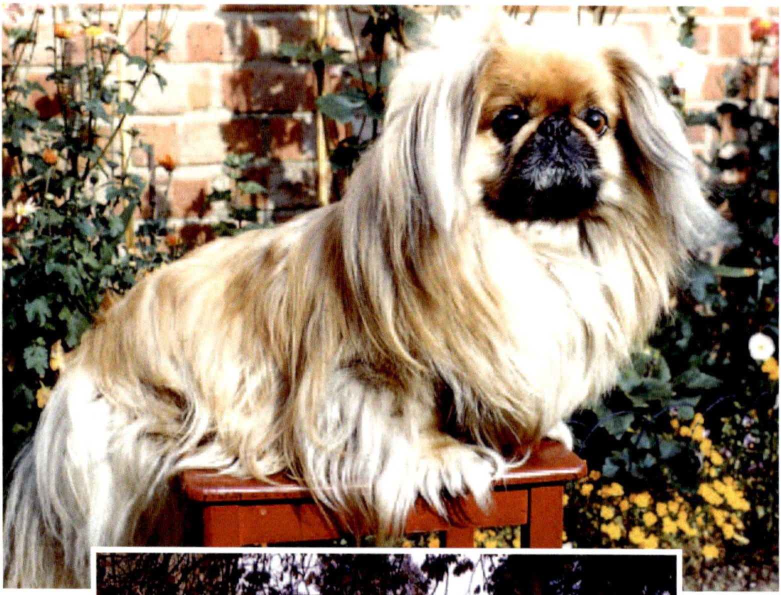
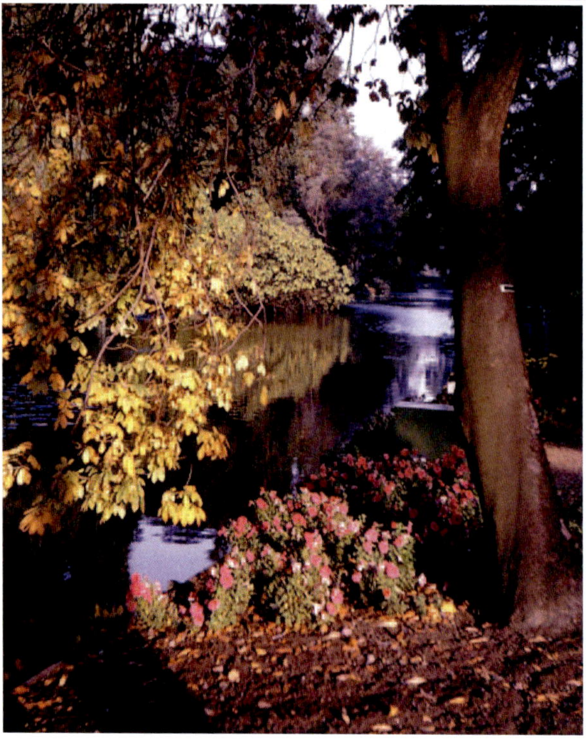

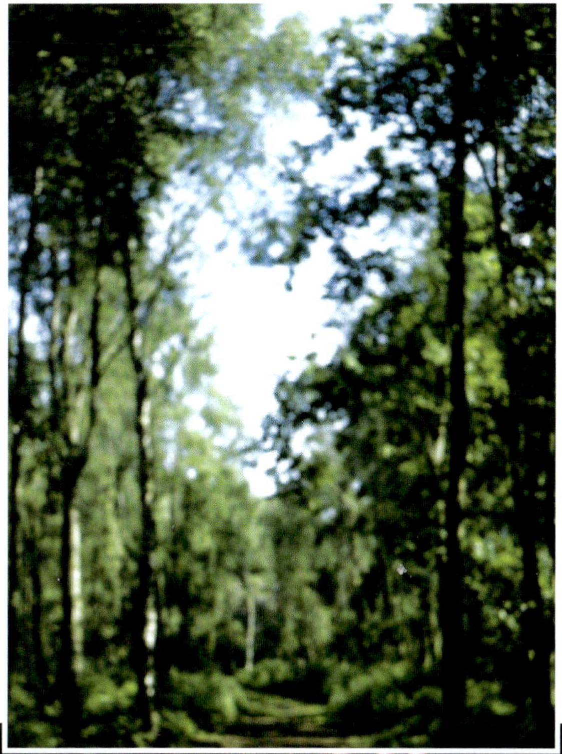

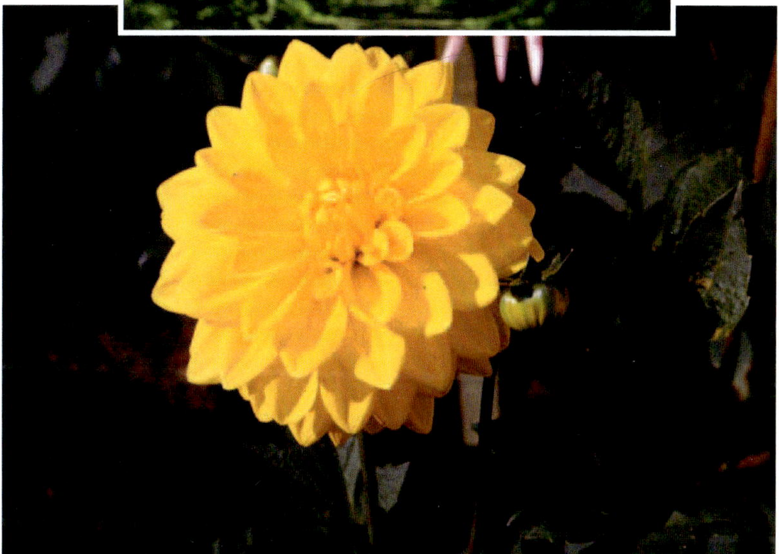

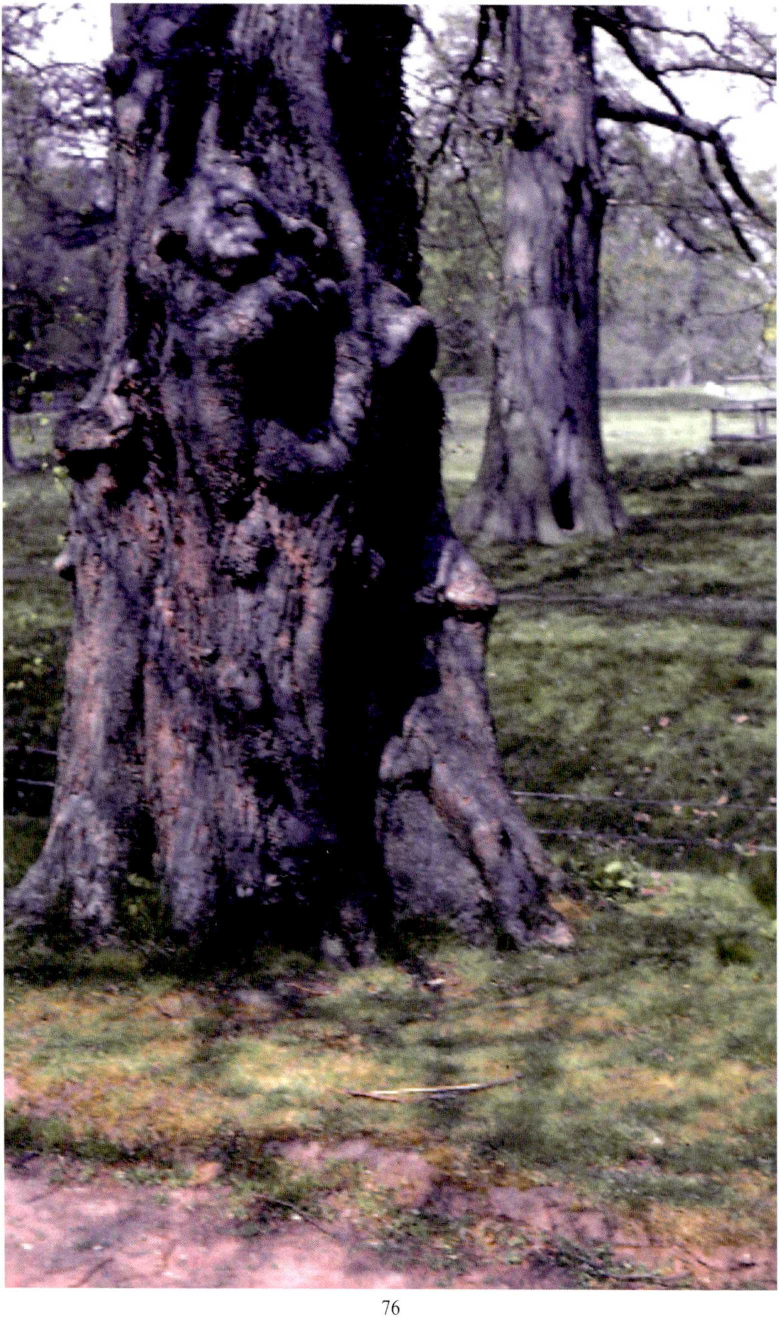

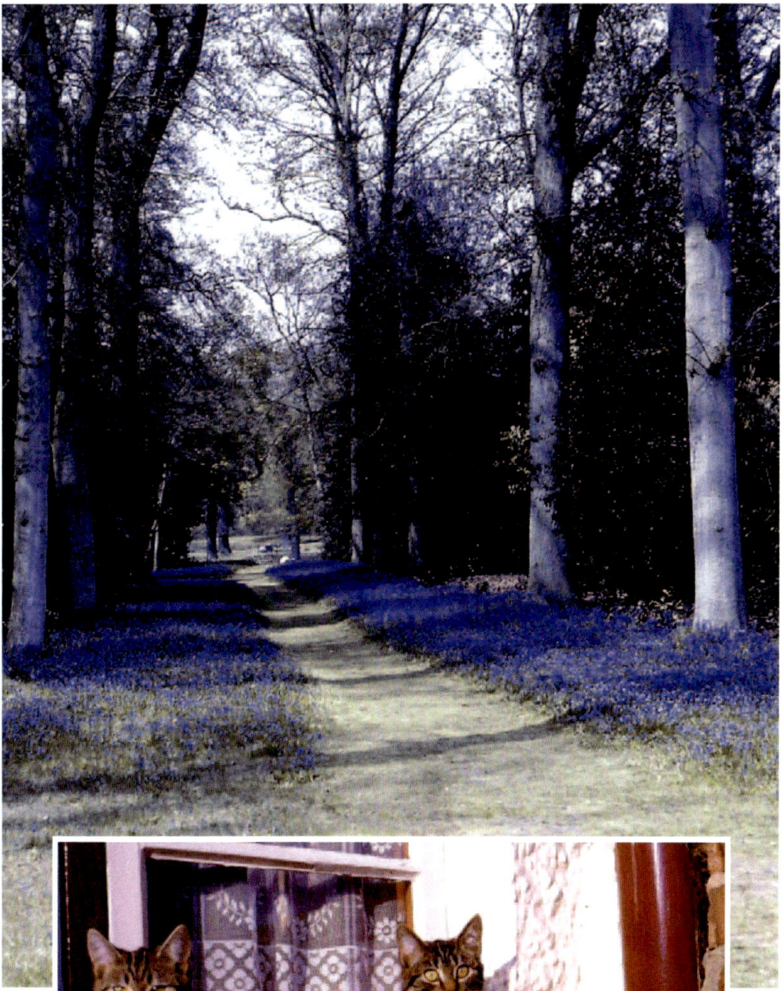

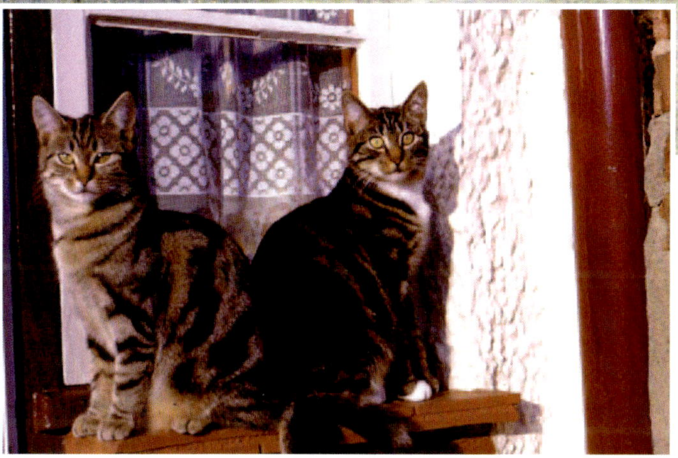

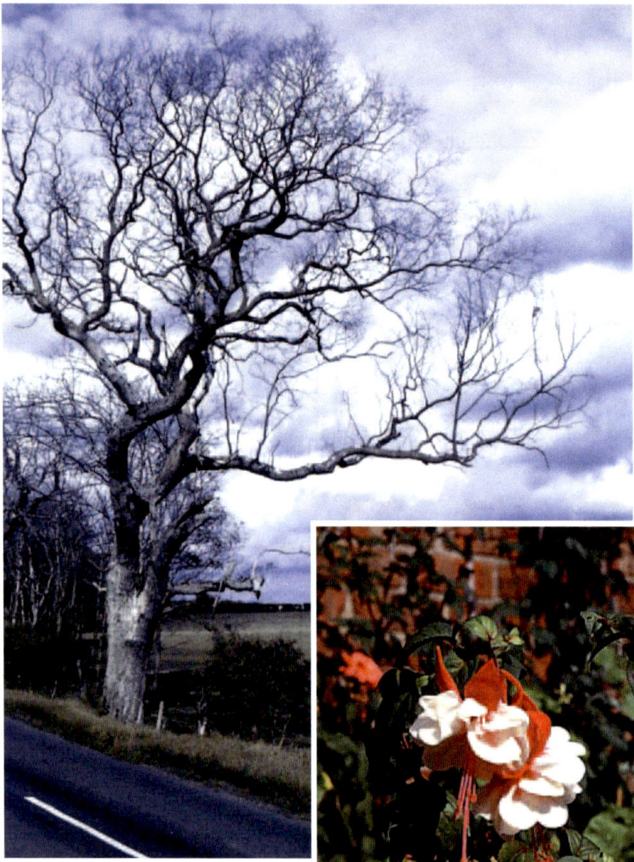

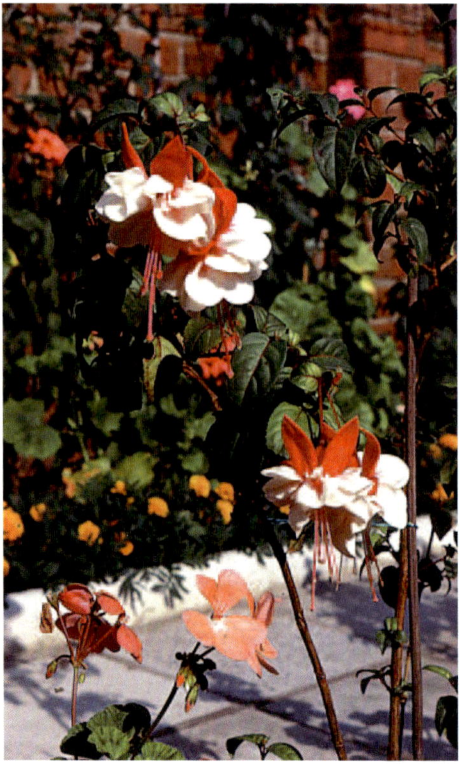

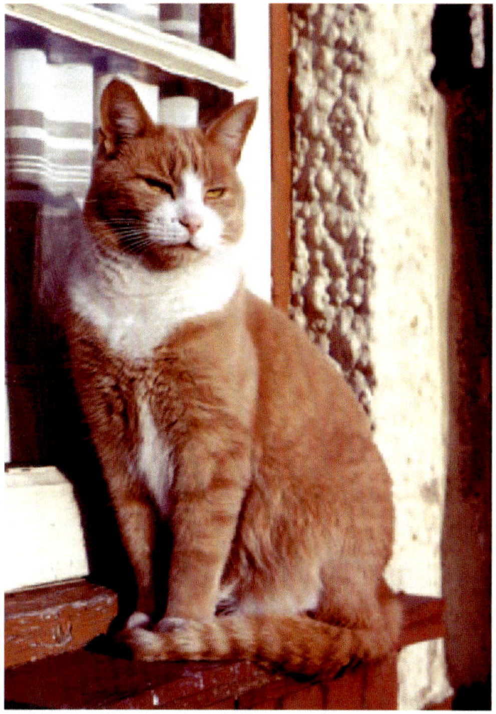
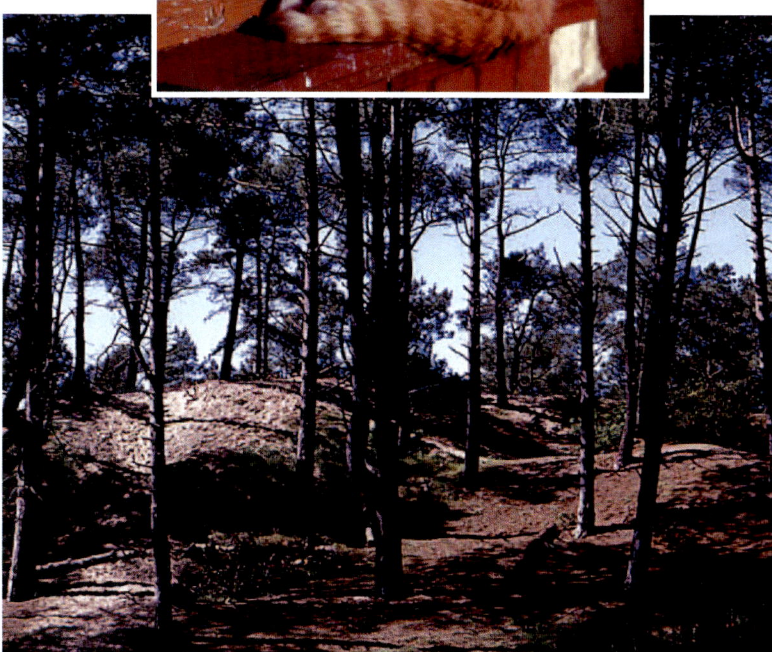

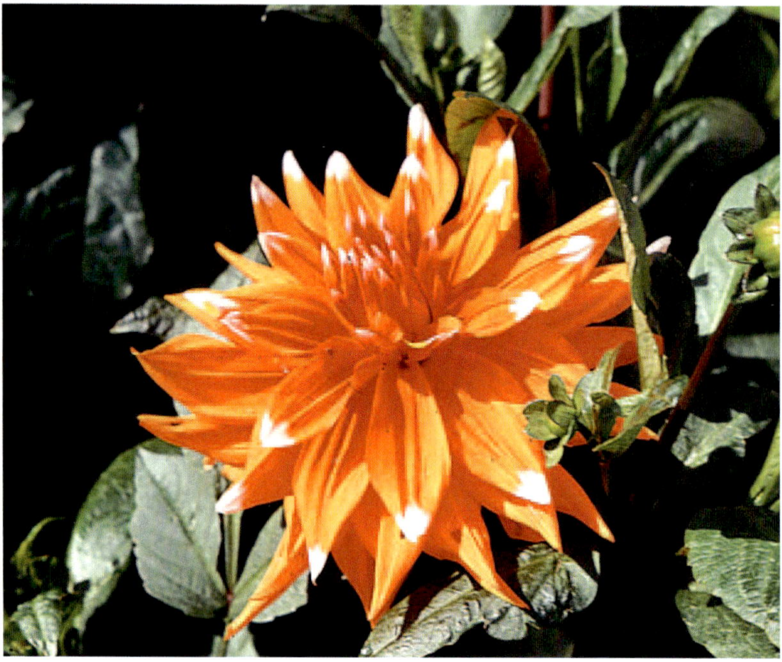

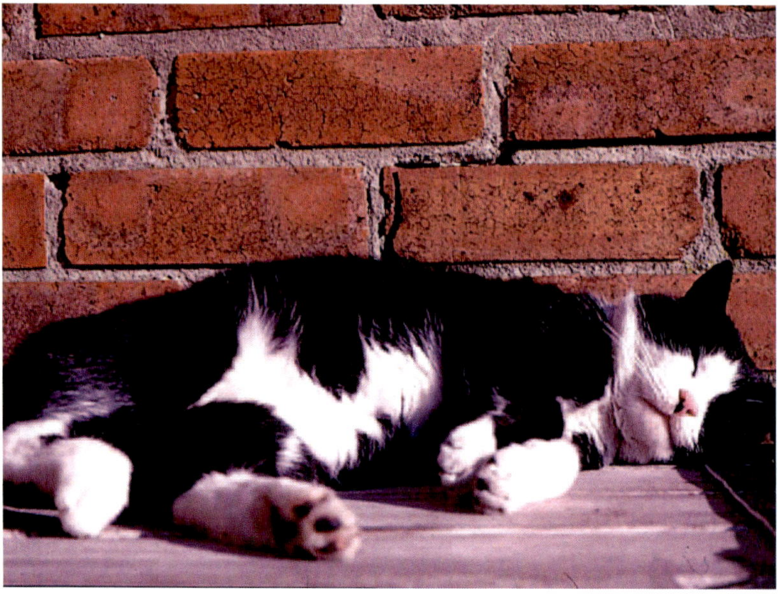

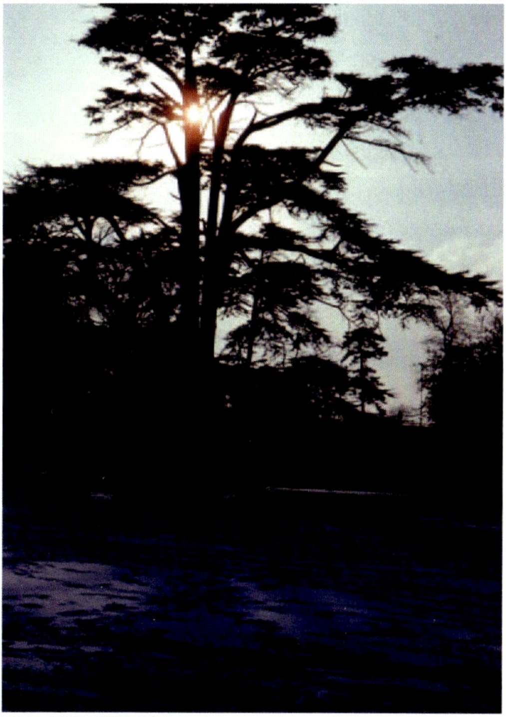

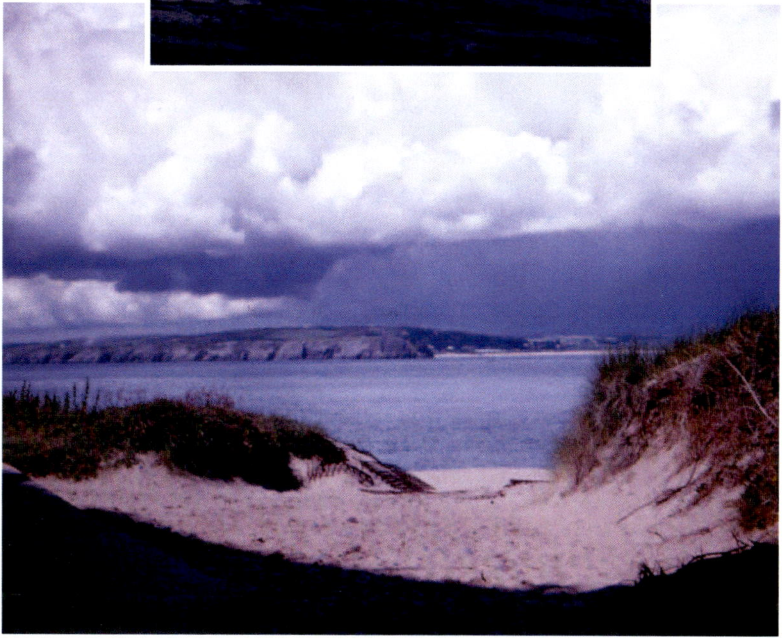

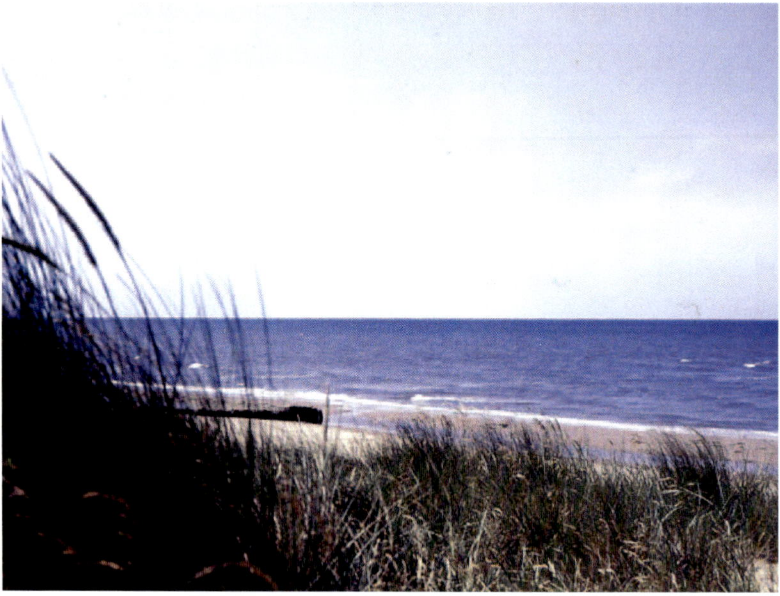

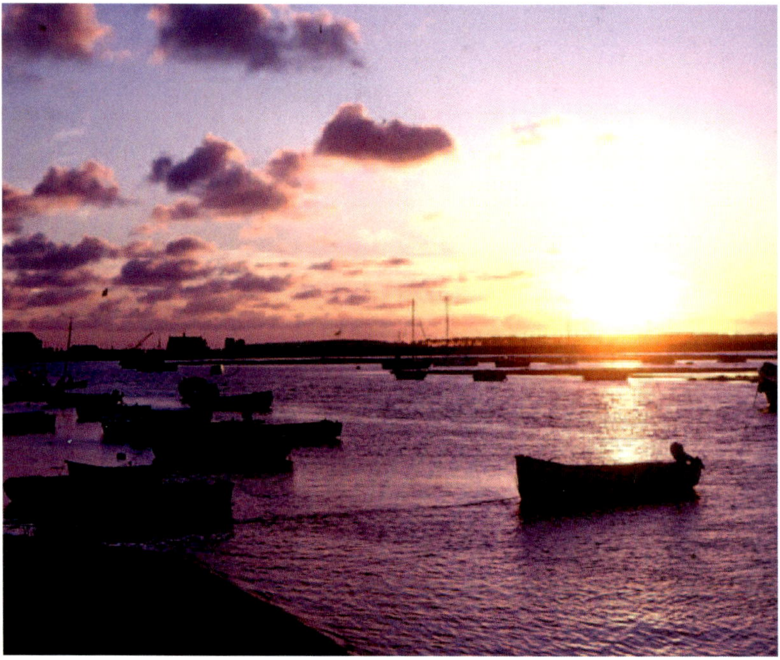

# *The Poems*

## *Chrysalis*

Night, folding dense around the speeding train,
Presses its formless dark upon the senses,
Unfathomable, as the future seems.
The timid heart shrinks back,
Clinging to the light.

But now the bridge across the darkling water,
And night is dazzled by a thousand gems
As light, no longer by the train contained,
Is flung upon the lake's reflecting surface,
Threading with diamond embroidery
Its white lace frill of ice.

The timid heart is drawn,
Waking to beauty – hinted – half disclosed,
By light escaping from its own cocoon,
Tempted – compelled – to struggle forth a wing.

## *Haiku 1*

Few would know the gem
Rich in its vibrant beauty
Once was a humble rock.

## Night Lights

I do not close the blinds. In the soft dark
I watch the lights invade my tiny space,
The fleeting headlights swing their amber glow
From wall to wall.

Flaring and fading, tossed by goblin shadows,
They mix, they part, sweeping, dipping, soaring;
From east, from west they silently collide,
Or shriek to stillness.

My ceiling a screen for fancied images,
Fluid and fastly changing; there are seas,
Rivers and mountains, shimmering images
Where deserts thirst.

Then sleep will close my eyes to fantasies,
But only changes daydreams into dreams.

## Age Speaks to Death

I have grown old, my roots are deep,
The dear familiar gives my heart content.
Leave me to rest awhile, here is home,
The day is not spent, I do not wish to sleep.

## *Dance With Me*

Come dance with me,
Out where the summer night
Has folded away the day,
Fresh from the dawn's unveiling.

Where lawns are soft awash
With moonlight's flooding,
Bathe in the gentle flow, unclad,
Untrammelled, as the naked sprites
That dance the woodland, taking for raiment
Scarves of gossamer and blue
Spun from the twilight's mist.

Dance with me and love me,
To the pure rhapsody of love's composing,
Under our feet the rhythm of creation.
Come where the throbbing turf is cushion-soft
And perfume from the rose and lavender,
Scattered by the evening's dew,
Clings to the grasses.

And if I kiss you,
Down where reflected stars
Dance on the mirror surface of the stream,
Feeling your fire with mine
Consume our hearts,
Only the reeds will listen,
Only the nightowl see.

## *The Loneliness of Today*

He stands unmoving,
Bowed by the burden of his many years.
He stands alone, his gaze on the distant hills
That blur the sky beyond the valley floor.
He looks but he does not see.
His eyes are empty,
His veins are empty of all conscious life,
Numb to the wind, to the sun, to birdsong.

They told him that morning,
Gone was the last to share the world he knew,
No more the fleeting hand-clasp.
Now there were no tomorrows,
No more yesterdays,
Only the aching aloneness
Of every today.

## *I Remember the Flowers*

I shed a tear or two,
There was no-one else to do it.
But what I remember most are the flowers

Crammed in a jamjar by the brown-stained sink,
Grey, withered, featureless,
Their gentle sweetness lost, as hers, perhaps,
Surrendered to decay.

How they had come to be there none may tell,
Their fragile beauty spoke of woods and hedgerows
Remote from here, where man's creative vision
Sowed only fields of concrete, growth of brick.

To one whose pleasures passed with yesterday,
What had they brought, what half-remembered joy?
But they had died, life-giving water spent,
Leaving slime traces on the grime-smeared glass.

She lay in grubby underwear, across the grubby bed,
Arthritic, old and frail; unlovely and unloved.
Neglect, perhaps, had been her killer, too.

## Freedom

Fly, little wild one, fly,
The bars of your cage are broken,
I have torn them apart.

Flutter bewildered wings, soar, rest on the wind,
Cleave the resistant air in wild uncharted flight,
Heart tremulous with unbelieving joy,
While rapture chokes your song.

Lost to my sight and to my hearing now
I weep: joy for my joy, grief for my grief.
Could I but share your freedom, your escape.
The sky is limitless, the sky is yours.
My wings are bruised, my wild heart long exhausted.
Invisible as hangs the cage of duty,
Never were stronger bars.

# Shy

You are dying.
You know it, and we know you know
But no-one speaks of it.

We have grown shy of you,
As someone set apart,
A stranger almost,
Lost the common ground we used to share:
Our far horizons.

Yours have grown near, no further now
Than these encircling walls
Enclosing all the small, familiar things
Of everyday.

Have these grown dear to you, the known to cling to
As the unknown looms?
We wonder, but we do not ask,
Cannot intrude.

'Good-bye' we say, 'see you tomorrow.'
'Yes' you say, knowing it might not be.
We know it might not be, but we are shy
And no-one speaks of it.

# Haiku 2

Bird sings to the snow
While its mate dies quietly
In their frozen nest.

## *The Trees are Bare*

Today the trees are bare.
A day but gone
Reluctant leaves still blurred their outline,
But today the trees are bare.

Skeletal and still,
Black as the raven's wing
Against a dove-grey sky,
The trees are bare.

Deep in the coma of suspended life,
Their feeble grasp
Has loosed the last frail links
With recent splendours,

Which now, mere remnants,
Prey of fussy ground-winds,
Husky in protest,
Are shuffled, tossed and scattered.

But blustering gales that whip the higher air,
Meeting scant hindrance,
Sweep through the naked boughs
With little stir.

All knowledge fallen with the falling sap,
They stand and wait,
Obedient to the earth's recurring cycle,
Nor know that they are waiting.

But in its season,
As the awakened pulse of living quickens,
Reborn awareness feels the swelling buds.
Tiny unfurling leaves
Clothing in haze-thin green
Each ebon branch. But now,
Today the trees are bare.

## November

November, and the cunning spider,
Hiding its talents through the summer hours,
Has overnight transformed my summer garden
Into a labyrinth of tangled ways,
Draping its deadly lace, dew-diamonded,
From stem to twig, from rose to lavender,
Cross and across my paths.

Low hung, the sun has gilded every common thing;
Even a brick is crafted out of beauty:
Russet and amber, overwashed with gold.
Geraniums throw their shadows on the wall,
Their naked flower heads, like giant spiders
With a hundred legs,
Climb and fall back as fickle winds decree.

The tired hedges welcome the autumn winds,
To lift the weight of grime-encrusted leaves,
Shunting them into drifts beside the pathways,
A rustling delight for little feet.
Safe in soft dust beneath their matted branches,
The chrysalis sleeps,
And in their roots the tiny burrowing mouse
Secretes its winter store.

## *The Golden Tree*

I buried you beneath the golden tree,
My little golden darling,
Where you had loved to spend the golden hours,
And all my days were sunshine.

The March winds grieve its branches with lament.
It weeps its golden blossom,
A pool of golden tears upon the grass,
And all my days are shadow.

The day you did not hear the morning call,
Nor waken to the loving of my touch,
I buried you beneath the golden tree.

## *A Brief Hiatus*

To Tommy Twist, his friends all said,
'It's more than time that you got wed,
Go find yourself a loving wife
And settle down to married life.'

To Tommy Twist, his wild oats sown
And tired of living on his own,
The idea held a strong attraction
And galvanised him into action.

He cast a calculating eye
On many damsels, far and nigh,
But interest in his intent
Was nowhere very evident.

*Continued over ...*

Now Bessie Bounce, long past her best,
Was also on the marriage quest,
But her expanding chest and waist
Were not to everybody's taste.

Meeting by chance, this hapless pair
Confessed a common goal to share,
And after due deliberation
Decided on collaboration.

But matrimony is no joke
And Tommy was a cautious bloke –
He wanted proof of what he'd got
Before he rushed to tie the knot.

And so they built a little nest
To put relations to the test,
Hopeful that they might discover
Kindred souls in one another.

Then Bessie, mindful of her mum,
('The way to his heart is through his tum')
Fed him on exotic dishes,
Irrespective of his wishes,

Weird and wonderful collations
From the cooks of many nations.
Tom's stomach longed for common grub,
The sort you'd find in any pub.

When she went out to buy a wok
He kissed goodbye and changed the lock.
The interlude a brief hiatus,
He settled back to single status.

## *A Non-Valentine*

Patricia's quite delightful
In slinky velvet clad,
Matilda's rather frightful,
But has a wealthy dad.

There's Geraldine and Stella,
Karen, Sylvia and Bella,
And little Mary Burton is a pet.
I could fall for Polly Tinker
But Big Beryl is a stinker –
I wouldn't want to fall into her net.

That just about sums up the present class,
But none of them would want to pair with me –
I'm very plain and spotty, as you see,
And so this year, St. Valentine, I pass.

## *Inconsistancy*

You lie to me
With every melting look and soft caress,
With every honeyed word and tender kiss.
How many others know your sweet embrace?
You come and go,
Fickle as April's sun.
And when you come here, radiant in your youth,
Telling your lies in word and touch and glance,
Then I will listen, as I always do,
Hoping one day, perchance, they may be true.

# *Limericks*

Said the rabbit to wife Ermintrude,
'Please forgive me if I'm being rude,
But I humbly request
That you give it a rest,
For we do have a very large brood.'

A handsome young vendor of wares,
Who attracted all feminine stares,
When asked for a kiss
By one pretty miss,
Said 'I only sell apples and pears.'

There once was a dealer in cars,
Who set off to find business on Mars,
But alack and alas
He ran out of gas
And never got further than Brighton.

There was a young lady of Ealing
Who walked like a fly on the ceiling.
When at last she fell down
She remarked with a frown,
'It's a most disagreeable feeling.'

Said a fish to the rest of his clan,
'I'm too fly for that simpleton, man.'
But the boast sounded weak
When the fly in his cheek
Had landed him right in the pan.

There once was a gardener named Stubb
Who fertilised all of his grub,
Till one day he grew roots
Through the soles of his boots,
So they planted him out like a shrub.

## *Cuthbert*

Tied to Mummy's apron strings,
Cuthbert never spread his wings,
'Til at the age of five and forty,
Having never once been naughty,
Cuthbert threw away his dummy,
Cut the strings and strangled Mummy.

## *Suspension*

There is ice on the pond,
Darkly transparent, crumpled with white creases.
Fallen leaves which yesterday
Jostled in thrusting winds,
Float captured in utter stillness.

Rebuffed by strange, unyielding water,
Ducks huddle, with ruffled plumage,
Motionless under the frost-rimed skeletons
Of bushes, lost to recognition
In winter's anonymity.

Into this capsule of suspended life
No noises penetrate.
With sound comes movement. Here,
Even the earth's strong heartbeat
Quietens to undetection and Nature, herself,
Pauses with bated breath.

# Lovely is My Love

They say my love is plain. What do they know
Of beauty, who only judge by sight?
She does not have a model's lissom grace,
Nor damask cheek; nor rosy, pouting lips
Nor flowing curls. (All wealth which time will squander).
Instead she has a breast that offers comfort,
A smile of tenderness, a gentle touch.
With confidence the kitten seeks her shoulder,
The toddler clings to her knee,
Drawn by the magnet of her warm compassion.
And there is laughter, too, in eyes that joy
In each small miracle – the opal raindrop
And the glow-worm's torch.
What if she does not charm the critic's eye,
The beauty of the soul needs no embellishing.

# Valentine

Oh, Valentine, I love you dearly,
Madly, deeply and sincerely.
I love your eyes, your lips, your hair –
In fact, I love you everywhere –
But while these joys to bliss amount,
I love far more your bank account.

# Puffball

A dandelion clock, A puffball.
I loved to blow it when I was a child,
To count the hours, and see the tasselled seed-specks fly,
Released, to dance the wind.

She sat in a row in front, her silver hair,
Fresh from the salon,
Like a ball of floss.
I wondered what would happen if I blew

# Pebble

The Chinese proverb, couched in wisdom, says
You can ignore a pebble in your pocket,
But put it in your shoe and you are crippled.

This pebble, satin smooth,
Rounded and polished by abrasive sand
And pounding seas of countless centuries,
Trapped instant agony inside my shoe,
But fondled in my hand, soothing, consoling,
As once Victorians
Would hold a worry egg to temper stress,
Persuades my nervous fingers to relax.

What was your origin, my little gem?
No common rock; limestone, basalt, flint.
Onyx? Chalcedony? Carnelian?
Warm to my touch as amber,
Holding a captured glow when lifted to the sun.

So with my cares.
Observing Chinese wisdom,
I drop them with my pebble in my pocket.

# Barney's Shop

Not so very long ago
(Just a hundred years or so)
Barney Bertie Blenkinsop
Kept a little corner shop.

On its shelves were many things:
Padlocks, pegs and curtain rings,
Joints of beef and ladies' slippers,
Snuff and rice and pairs of kippers.

There were broomsticks made for witches,
Skipping ropes and small boys' britches,
Pills to cure coughs and colic,
Eggs and soap and strong carbolic.

There were mops and peas in packets,
Lamps and cakes and children's jackets,
Pails and polish, bags of coffee,
Spades and pens and treacle toffee.

People came to buy his wares,
Wanted screws or socks or chairs,
Yards of lace or gents' straw hats,
Cooking pots or fireside mats.

Barney always shook his head.
They were not for sale, he said –
Wouldn't sell a single button,
Ladies' gloves or piece of mutton.

Not a thing would Barney sell,
Not a clothes-line nor a bell,
Not a buckle nor a pin,
Nor a bowl for washing in.

This was odd, the people thought –
If his goods could not be bought,
Why did Barney Blenkinsop
Keep his little corner shop?

It was rumoured he would sell
To the folk from Goblin Dell,
Little men with rosy faces,
Wearing beards and boots and braces.

Passing Barney's shop at night
Folks could often see a light,
Glimpsed the men by candle-glow
But none would see them come or go.

In that village to this day
You will hear the people say,
Once a Barney Blenkinsop
Kept the little corner shop.

But he would not sell his wares,
Not his apples nor his pears,
Bales of cloth nor balls of string,
Not a bit of anything.

Then his shop was shut one day –
Barney B. had gone away,
Went off with the little men
And was never seen again.

## *Poor Minnie Mouse*

'Now don't you go too far away,'
Said Mrs Mouse to Minnie,
'And don't fall over in the mud
And dirty your clean pinny.'

'And if you see a pussy cat
Run home as quick as quick,
And don't eat any cheese you find –
You know it makes you sick.'

'Don't play too near the lily-pond
In case you tumble in,
And don't play on the rubbish-heap
In the empty treacle tin.'

'Don't play with nasty Robert Rat,
Don't tease the hedgehog, Winnie.'
'So many things I mustn't do,
I won't go out,' said Minnie.


## *Haiku 3*

He mends the poor's shoes.
He knows they cannot pay him;
He walks bare-footed.

## *One Friday Afternoon*

Old Nell, she was a donkey, who
Was owned by Farmer Brown,
And every Friday afternoon
She took the cart to town.

She was so very quiet and good
And knew the way so well,
That Farmer Brown just went to sleep
And left it all to Nell.

Now as Nell reached the market-place
One afternoon in June,
She saw a monkey dancing
To a barrel-organ tune.

The monkey wore a yellow cap
And little coat of red –
He jumped and danced about the road
And stood upon his head.

A crowd had gathered round to watch,
And when Old Nell came by,
The monkey threw his cap at her
And hit her in the eye.

And then he jumped upon her back,
Which gave her such a start
That poor Old Nell sprang in the air,
And over went the cart.

*Continued over ...*

The farmer woke up with a shock
As to the ground he fell,
And when he scrambled to his feet
He looked around for Nell.

Old Nell was galloping down the road
With the monkey holding tight,
And people in the market-place
Scattered to left and right.

After her went Farmer Brown
(He was too fat to run),
And danced about and shouted out –
Oh dear, it was such fun.

The organ-grinder shouted, too,
And after them he ran
To try to get his monkey back,
And so the race began.

Nell and the monkey set the pace,
Next came the organ-man.
A crowd of people followed him,
And last the farmer ran.

And so they ran all through the town
And out the other side,
And in a field in front of her
A duck-pond Nell espied.

Thought Nell, 'I'll teach a lesson to
This naughty chimpanzee,
For it was very rude of him
To throw his cap at me.'

So over to the pond she ran
And halted suddenly,
And bent her head, and over it
Splash! Went the bad monkey.

He couldn't swim a little bit
But squealed and splashed about,
And was so very frightened
That at last Nell fished him out.

She grabbed him by his coat of red
And dropped him on the shore,
And it is very certain that
He'll play his tricks no more.

And then Nell turned and trotted back
To meet old Farmer Brown,
And taking him upon her back
She ambled back to town.

The farmer did his marketing,
And straightened out the cart,
And in a very little while
For home they made a start.

And still on Friday afternoons
Nell trots along to town –
And in the cart, quite peacefully,
Sleeps good old Farmer Brown.

## Kathy

We will not say goodbye,
You haven't left us,
Only slipped quietly behind the veil
Our mortal vision cannot penetrate.
And we will know you in the gentle places
Of our minds,
And feel your presence when our hearts reach out,
Only a step away.

## Fragment

Quietness, like a silken shadow
Slips over, under and between,
Leaving no place for raucous noise to linger.
Now peace is vibrant with the steady throb
Of Nature's heartbeat
And filled with gentle breathing from the trees
The quivering grasses whisper.

## The Meadow Fairy

There are fairies in the meadow,
Playing in the sun,
For I saw them there this morning
And I spoke to one.

Such a dainty little creature,
Dabbling in the dew.
I took off my hat and, bowing,
Said 'Good-day to you.'

But she wouldn't stay to gossip,
Spread her wings in flight
And, before I could detain her,
Disappeared from sight.

## *Paradise, Once*

Few know this place, or if they did,
Paid scant regard to it.
This little hollow where the sand-dunes dip
And rise again, their flowing undulations
Barely acknowledging the minor interruption.
Perhaps a path here, once,
Assisted scrambled access to the shore,
But it was long forgotten, long disused,
Long overgrown with blackberry and thorn.
Here was my childhood's secret paradise,
A refuge from the alien adult world.
Here, in this sun-trapped solitude, breathless with silence,
I passed the blissful hours.
Hot sand was firm but yielding under me,
Limitless the azure sky above.
I swam with my dreams, away and away in its vastness.
Over my head the dunes rose high, tiny white puff-ball clouds
Caught in their crowns of marram grass and thistles.
A hedge of briar screened the fields below.
Butterflies, pale-winged, lethargic,
Fluttered and rested on pink campion
And on sea holly, where it clung to small wind-sculpted crevasses,
And beetles charged at unseen enemies,
Their burnished armour gleaming.
How it has shrunk. Those once towering dunes
I can now scale in half a dozen strides.
The sand is grubby; never has cleaning tide
Breached the dunes' defences.
Was it this litter-strewn when I was young?
Oh, for the child's eyes that saw only beauty.

# *The Only Permanence*

One thing eternal,
One only permanence:
Silence.

Silence entire and absolute
Man cannot know.
The drowning silence when there was no earth,
When there was void,
A nothing, vast and limitless,
And stillness
Beyond a man's conceiving.

Our silences are full of murmurings,
Our very selves deny them purity;
We breathe, pulsate:
Movement is sound, there is no stillness
Absolute,
Though ears may not be tuned
To catch the whispered stirrings.

Silence was shattered when the world was born.
No gentle coming, this – no quiet dawning.
An infant full of angry bellowing,
Of ceaseless fret.
Chaos and turbulence its swaddling clothes,
Discord and thunder-roll its lullaby.
Noise, huge and purposeless, unleashed, undisciplined:
A maelstrom of unfettered sound.
Noise like a deluge,
Like a sweeping tide
Rising, engulfing, all-pervading noise.

But noise succumbed with passing time to music;
Like Hope emerging from Pandora's box
Came music,
Mesmerising sound,
Threading its strands throughout the wilderness,
Breathing faint patterns on the troubled air:
And Chaos stayed its rampaging to hearken.
Drawn by invisible magnetic strings,
Tempered and disciplined;
Falling to silences between vibrating chords,
The air breath-caught in intervals of playing.
But silences that cling to sounds of earth.

When Earth, like all created things,
Long stripped of life,
Decays, disintegrates
And falls, fragmented, to oblivion,
Leaving to stillness the unfathomed void,
There will be silence,
Silence profound and infinite,
The undisputed All,
The only permanence.

## Haiku 4

The battle was done.
Silence lay over the dead,
Then a small bird sang.

## Haiku 5

Tears are but raindrops
Washing the clouds from the sky
Revealing the sun.

## *They Do Not Come Here*

They do not come here.
People do not come,
Only the seabird and the sidling crab,
And waves that tease the shingle from the strand.

Sweet isolation from the faceless ones
That seethe and fester on the city's streets,
Killing the soft sweet air with poisoned breath,
Beating discordant clamour on the brain.

They do not come here.
Only the marram stirs
And sunlight tiptoes round the jagged rocks
Where seaweed eddies gently in the pools.

Peace and her twin, the shy Tranquillity,
Fleeing the turbulence of the faceless ones,
Breathe benediction on this solitude,
And silence throbs like music in the ear.

They do not come here.
People do not come.

## *Haiku 6*

Winter strips the leaves,
Buds are dormant. The tree weeps,
Forgetting the spring.

## *The Worst Winter*

We were young then,
When it started we were young.
We had not known the deep, relentless cold
When sullen, lowering skies denied the sun:
A cold that gripped and shook,
A cold that paralysed,
That penetrated with the piercing wind,
A keening wind that numbed the heart with grieving.

We shivered, breathless, when the storms swept in;
And there were many storms.
The clouds built mountains, layer upon layer,
Sable and grey, towering, ominous,
Forming vast caverns where the thunder echoed
Before it crashed its fury overhead
And lightning flung its shafts at many places –
We saw where crimson smudges stained the sky.

When there were storms the winds were fierce with heat,
A choking, searing heat that did not warm.
We sweated then,
The clammy sweat of fear.
Even our tears were cold.
We wept for death,
The death of innocence, of dreams, of beauty.

How long, that winter?
Who can tell how long?
We did not measure time.
We saw, at last, the clouds disperse like vapour;
A timid sun, new born, braved a pallid sky,
And it had ended then,
That winter made by man. But we –
We were no longer young.

# *The Mountain*

He came to where they dwelt upon the plain,
Where the wide river, slumberous, barely stirred.
They were a lowly folk of humble needs:
Sober, passive and unquestioning.

He came to them because they had the mountain,
As others had done before him.
Eagerness was dancing in his eyes
And laughter on his lips.

The mountain's summit cleaved the arching sky
And, in reflection, pierced the river's depth,
Sun-silvered blade of ice.
Stark, grey, precipitous its towering sides,
With massive boulders on its lower slopes,
Flung from its shoulders in some ancient fury
Long centuries ago,
Lying moss-green amid the gold of faded grasses,
Where light and shadow glanced
Or slipped away behind the stunted trees.

The mountain was their everyday familiar,
Always and doubly in their consciousness –
In vivid, powerful reality
And in the glassy river's imagery.
Respect they had; no one of them would trespass
Upon its sanctity,
This mountain of so many mysteries,
Where spirits dwelt that sent the angry thunder
To tear the breathless air,
Slashing the clouds with jagged, fiery light,
And set the earth to tremble.

He left them, and they watched him go
Silently.
He left them to climb the mountain,
As others had done before him.
None had ever come down.

## Haiku 7

*Spring*
    The sapling breaks bud
    To greet spring, fed by dead leaves
    From last year's budding.

*Summer*
    The summer shower
    Does not please the sun-seeker
    But gladdens dry earth.

*Autumn*
    Squirrels bury nuts
    But when dead leaves have fallen
    Lose their hiding-place.

*Winter*
    When icy winds rage
    People wrap in warm clothing
    But the trees stand bare.

## *Usually People Tether Goats*

Once, in a country lane, I saw
Five goats.
Usually people tether goats.

Charming and witless creatures, there
They stood,
Troubled, uncertain, gazing here and there,
Cropping the wayside grass or making little rushes
To butt each other, though without aggression,
Stamping their little hooves, tossing their heads
And bleating at the sky.

By six-o'-clock my outer office room
Has long been empty.
Holding its breath, unwonted peace creeps in.

Five cluttered desks, five scattered, lonely chairs,
Five overspilling wastebins, all that now
Remain as witness to the toilsome hours.

Mine the juniors, untrained as yet,
Undisciplined, one step removed from school:
Still liable to little bursts of temper,
Finding frustration in their ignorance,
Striving to run before they learn to walk.
They weary me with idiot complaints.

Their bleating voices now have died away,
The sound of stamping feet lost to the echo
Which fills the exit corridor.
Charming, foolish, vulnerable souls,
Released into a world they hardly know.

# *Metamorphosis*

Charlie loved to go to Town,
To saunter up the Strand and down,
Throwing off domestic fetters,
Rubbing shoulders with his betters.

Walked The Mall with languid pace,
Haughty smile upon his face,
Tilted bowler, spats and brolly,
Just the dog for any folly.

Back inside his humble house
He became a hen-pecked mouse:
'Yes, dear, no dear,' to his wife –
Anything for peaceful life.

She was big and she was brassy,
Just the opposite of classy,
Had her spouse where she intended;
Least he said was soonest mended.

And so, when he was feeling down,
Charlie took himself to Town,
Strolled the parks and trod the squares,
Basking in admiring stares.

In imagination he
Revelled in debauchery,
Aped the role of shameless sinner
Then went home to cook the dinner.

## *The Call of The Sea*

Is not this place the haven of delight?
These low-browed hills, this sandy waste of shore
Whereon, forever ceaseless, day and night
The giant waves in kingly splendour roar.

They pant, they growl, they call me more and more;
They beckon from the traffic in the Strand.
From desk and ledger comes a mocking roar –
I see the crested waves on every hand.

I dream, I work a little – dream again,
And see a distant, barren, windswept shore.
How can I concentrate on business men,
The endless questions from the office door?

I am not in the world of cares and woes,
The everlasting toil for daily bread.
My heart is wandering where the sea-breeze blows,
And where the rippled sand-bed is, I tread.

The white gulls dip and splash and send their cry
To welcome me to share their lone domain;
A school of porpoise sportively pass by
Along a green and mystic deep-sea lane.

Go to your Devon with its scenery grand,
Which poets worship and which bards extol.
Its brilliant colours and its rugged land
They love, and into wordy praise enrol.

Give me the solitude of Norfolk shores,
A blue-grey sky – a drift of summer rain,
And keep your gorse, your heather and your moors,
Your laughing fields – the sea has called again.

## *Farewell My Love*

Dear, I must leave you now;
The golden day
Sinks into twilight's arms, and soon
Night will enfold them in her velvet cloak,
Safe from the prying moon.

Relinquished are my dreams of promised joy:
No more the dawn,
Reaching pale fingers through the fading night
With soft caress will wake me from my slumber
To rise and come with eager heart to you.

The barque long since has left the distant harbour –
I see its shadow where the sun's bright rim
Fades now to amber, now to palest gold.
Darkling and silent on the swelling water,
Full-rigged in sable, swifter than the wind,
It comes with Fate unyielding at the helm.

And I must meet it, where the ebon prow
Cleaves the fine shingle,
Tossing in bounty moon-white pearls of spray.

These things you cannot see,
Life clouds your eyes.
Do not forget , but do not grieve me long;
Life calls to life, with death it cannot bide.
Your sands have long to run.

So, dear, I leave you now,
The ebb is urgent and the sailors call
And I must answer.
Thus I must speak my final word to you,
Farewell.